His Greatest Catch

No Ordinary Family Book 4

LINDA BARRETT

DEDICATION

To my wonderful sons and daughters-in-law—
Great catches, all!

Cover art by Shelley Kay at Web Crafters

E-book and print formatting by Web Crafters

www.webcraftersdesign.com

CHAPTER ONE

Robert and Grace Delaney
Heaven
The Universe

Dear Mom and Dad,

Do you know what a shrink is? I visit a shrink every week now, but I don't talk a lot. I'd rather talk to you, so writing is better. I miss you so much. We all do. Can you hear us talking down here on Earth? Emily thinks you can. So, every night, she plays Amazing Grace on her violin. Just for you, Mom.

Dad, remember how you played catch with Brian and me in the backyard every night? Well, now we're baseball players—we're on leagues every spring and summer. I wish you could coach! Or at least be in the stands and see us play.

I'm mostly sad inside, but sometimes, I'm more mad than sad. Stupid accident! Stupid ice! Only one thing is good. Brian and me. We stick together. I'm glad we're twins.

I love you to pieces. Maybe one day, I'll hit a home run all the way to heaven.

Your son,
Andy

P.S. I'll write again soon.

Eleven-year-old Andrew Delaney folded the letter and searched his oldest sister's desk for an envelope and stamp. He knew exactly where to look. Writing had become a habit, and he was happy Lisa always had stamps lying around.

He walked into the hallway and slipped the envelope amid the outgoing mail where no one would notice it.

Twenty-one years later…

Boston liked its holiday weather crisp and clear, and that was just fine with Andrew Delaney. He inhaled the clean air with a quick nod of approval as he left the printing shop mid-afternoon and hoisted the heavy box to his shoulder. He'd become the family go-fer. *Reduced* to being the family go-fer. According to his sisters, it was his own fault for being single. He had more freedom to come and go at odd hours.

He chuckled, recalling how his mock complaints were laughed at by his family. Only his oldest sister, Lisa, had said, "you're not the go-fer, Andy. For this event, you're the *go-to* guy! We want to raise megabucks for the foundation." She still acted like a mom.

He didn't mind being the errand boy for next week's gala at all. The box he carried contained attractive program booklets honoring all donors as well as guests attending the affair, and had his seal of approval.

Any organization raising money for kids without parents would be at the top of the list for him. But this one was special. The *Robert and Grace Delaney Children's Foundation.* He and his siblings had created it in memory of their own parents and were on the board of directors.

He turned the corner and started down historic but trendy Newbury Street toward the parking lot where he'd left his SUV. People roamed up and down the block of brownstones, searching for the boutiques, eateries or specialty shops on their lists. Actually, a pretty sight full of colorful parkas, knit caps and the holiday sound of jingling bells and calls of good cheer. Shop doors opened and closed as he snaked his way toward his goal. Shouldn't all these shoppers be home cooking on the day before Thanksgiving and leave the sidewalks less crowded for him? Ha! Fat chance.

He began humming a holiday tune when the door of an art gallery on his left started to open. Moving to avoid it, he saw a woman trying to maneuver a baby stroller onto the street. He grabbed the door handle and held the door open.

"Thank you," she said, looking up at him. "Thanks a...lot." Her blue eyes narrowed. But he'd recognized her immediately.

"Shannon? Shannon Murphy?"

A smile slowly crossed her face; her eyes brightened. "Andy Delaney! How nice."

3

"And you're still batting a thousand. You never mixed Brian and me up back in high school," said Andy. "One of the few who didn't."

She pushed the carriage further onto the sidewalk, and he released the door. "Going my way?" she asked, maneuvering the stroller.

"Sure," he replied, not caring exactly where she was headed.

The carriage rocked. "Out, out," came a high-pitched voice.

"Whoa. That's sounds like a command." Andy peeked down at the toddler, noting the same blue eyes as her mom. "Cutie," he said.

"And a handful."

"And how old is this little handful?"

"Two-and-a-half. Actually, almost three. We're doing some errands today, and the gallery was on my list. A quick visit."

"Not a usual place for a baby carriage, huh?"

"Today wasn't usual. My holiday bonus was ready early and I was anxious to pick it up. I work there."

The baby looked at Andy, her eyes narrowing. "Mom-my?" she wailed.

Shannon leaned over the stroller. "This is Andy, honey. Andy is my friend."

"Fwend?"

"Yes. An old friend." She patted Andy's arm.

That's all it took for a change to occur. A smile appeared first, then the toddler raised her arms. "Mommy, up, up."

Once in Shannon's arms, Maddie studied Andy, then looked at her surroundings. "Doggy! Look, Mommy." She pointed, then exclaimed, "Two doggies!" She wriggled with excitement and caught Shannon by surprise.

"Back in the stroller for you, Maddie. We're almost at the car anyway." She leaned over the carriage.

"Hang on a sec. Let's give her a break," said Andy. "If you balance this box on the stroller, I'll carry her...if she'll come to me." He placed the box, then extended his arms. "Want to see more, Maddie?"

She glanced at her mother.

"It's okay. Remember, Andy's my friend."

Her smile inched across her face. "Up, Fwend. Up. Higher! See more."

Andy grinned back, and glanced at Shannon with his thumb up. "Wow! She's a great kid. Good common sense. Jen's twins trusted everybody. They needed a leash!" Glancing at Shannon's questioning look, he added. "Anyway, that's what Jen said. I'm innocent." He took the child from her mother. "Is this high enough, baby?"

"Not baby. Maddie!"

Shannon's soft laughter got to him. Sounded sweet and familiar. Like in the old days when they'd worked on the school newspaper together.

"Now, I know you're really Shannon Murphy. You always had the greatest laugh. Still do. Family life must agree with you."

The laughter stopped. Her eyes darkened. Something wasn't right and Andy braced himself for whatever she was about to say next.

"It's Roberts now. Shannon Roberts, but family life is only Maddie and me. I named her after her dad." She paused, then quietly said, "Matt died in Afghanistan without ever meeting her."

His breath caught, and Andy automatically took her hand and squeezed it, his heart heavy for her. "I'm terribly sorry, Shan. I see the stories on television...and I donate...but..."

5

"Yeah. It sucks. It really does. Oh..,Maddie's a wiggly worm, so hold on tight—like when you catch a fly ball at Fenway."

"Got it."

"Mommy...?

"I'm right here. Andy is holding you."

The baby looked down and studied him. "Andee..."

"Close enough. Do you know more words?"

She nodded fiercely and began singing. "Old Macdonna hadda farm. E I E I O. Cow! Moo moo, evewywhere a moo moo."

"So glad I asked," said Andy. "She could be a Delaney. In my family, everyone sings. It's unreal."

"I don't really know anyone in your family but you and Brian," she said, "so I'll take your word for it. Glad and amazed you both got what you wanted...Major League baseball. What are the odds?"

She gestured down the street. "Are we heading toward the same parking lot?"

"Seem to be," he replied, ignoring the career comment.

They started walking and the box shifted position. Shannon steadied it. "What's in here, Andy? It's pretty heavy."

He sighed. "Those are programs for the big gala we're putting on a week from Saturday night. A fundraiser for the memorial foundation in memory of my parents."

"I've heard about it," she said slowly. "My folks are going. I think they bought a whole table for Murphy Auto Parts with my two siblings and their spouses and of course, my grandfather. He loves to be in the thick of things."

Andy's mind raced like a car at the Daytona 500. "What about you? Can't you come?"

"I-I really haven't been going out yet…" She glanced up at her daughter, who seemed content to watch the world from on high.

"Maybe now's the time to consider it," said Andy, "if not for your sake, for mine."

"Yours?" she asked in surprise. "Mind explaining? Who, what, where, when, how and why?"

That newspaper experience seemed to have stuck. Andy took a moment to consider the details of the dinner-dance that meant so much.

"I'm going to be auctioned."

Her mouth opened and closed. "Could you repeat that?

"Part of this fundraiser is a bachelor auction. The most, and I quote, 'eligible bachelors in town.' Which evidently includes me. Plus a couple of other Red Sox players, a couple of physicians that Scott—my sister, Emily's husband—recruited, some CEOs and other high-profile Boston bachelors. We've got local radio personalities to do the announcing, but Mike will be the general emcee."

"Ah-h. Of course. Mike Brennan, your brother-in-law. How's the quarterback liking retirement?"

"Not retired. Just a change in careers. He's announcing for the Riders now instead of playing. So, whaddyasay, Shannon? Will you save me?"

Shannon remained quiet, but at least she hadn't said an outright no. "And I'll return the bid, of course," he added. "I don't expect you to lay out big bucks for this."

"I hadn't gotten that far in my thinking, but Andy. I'm sorry. I don't go out yet. Can't quite bring myself to rejoin a social singles world. I just kind of stick with my family."

He gave her a moment. "Then maybe it's time to reconsider," he said. "Maddie's almost three now. Is the right time when she's four? Five? Eighteen?"

He sensed her irritation but continued. "Before you know it, you'll be rocking on the porch of an old age home with a basket of yarn at your feet, knitting blankets! Think about it."

Her spontaneous laughter surprised him. Maybe surprised her as well.

"You really painted a picture there," she said. "I've already got the rocking chair. That's how I put Maddie to sleep some nights."

He glanced at the baby, who was sucking her thumb, still content to observe the world from on high. "You and she make quite a picture. A beautiful one."

"Are you trying to soften me up?" she asked, smiling. "Well, it worked. I'll...think about the auction and let you know." She stopped walking and searched her purse. "Here it is," she said, holding up her cell phone. "What's your number?"

Encouraged, he told her and whipped out his own phone from his jacket pocket. "An even exchange," he said, handing it to her. "Since my hands are full, will you..."

"Sure...but don't count on me, Andy. I'm not the same girl you once knew."

##

Shannon's high school memories of Andy Delaney kept her company as she drove up Commonwealth Ave to her less trendy neighborhood and turned onto Birch Street and into her own driveway. The Andy she'd just left at the parking lot—mature, handsome, confident—superimposed himself on that teenager of memory. More wiry and slender back then, of course, and quieter than his brother. He'd matured into an attractive man, still a friendly sort. Of course, he'd always had the confidence a gifted athlete carried. As center fielder for the Sox, his self-assurance could only have grown.

After turning off the car's engine, she opened the rear door as quietly as possible and removed a sleeping Maddie from her car seat, hoping her daughter would remain asleep for an hour or two more. Walking to her front door with keys in hand, she looked with satisfaction at the safe and homey world she'd created for her little family.

True, the clapboard, Cape-style house was small. In fact, it could be called tiny. But it was hers, thanks to her parents' help with the down payment. Not that she wanted to accept help, but her choices had been limited.

Move in with her folks? Stay in Texas on the military base? Her folks were great, but had she given in, she would have lost her independence. Her military family was also great, but too far from Boston. She couldn't, in good conscience, keep a brand-new baby away from all the grandparents. And she, herself, had been an emotional mess.

Her wonderful Matthew, an officer caught in an ambush by supposedly friendly locals. She should have been prepared; military wives lived with that fear every day. But grief had crushed her. She'd needed the love and support of her mom and dad, brother, sister and their families and her Pops.

So here she was, in her own place, with family nearby but not choking her. Life was as good and safe as it could be. Calm. Until a pair of gleaming green eyes popped into her mind. Her recent memory of the past hour.

A glitzy dinner-dance with a million people?

She shivered. No way. She preferred intimate gatherings.

A bachelor auction?

Definitely not her style. Besides, she didn't even own a fancy dress.

Andy had been a friend, but high school was a long time ago. She'd call him tomorrow and hope he'd understand her refusal.

Now she had to bake an apple pie and prepare dressing for tomorrow's turkey. Oh...dang! She couldn't call him on Thanksgiving.

She slipped off Maddie's winter jacket and kissed her soft cheek as she laid her in the crib. "Here's another one, from your daddy," she whispered and kissed the toddler again.

##

"Wow! What a mess. Where do you want this carton?" Andy stood in the center hall of his oldest sister's house on Beacon Street, the house he'd grown up in, not believing the disarray of stuff that greeted his eyes. Boxes everywhere. Papers piled on the coffee table. So unlike Lisa, who believed in organization.

"It's an organized mess," Lisa protested. "I know where everything is."

That he could believe. "What about everyone else? You know, the people who are supposed to help out here?"

"Just label the carton in big letters," she said, handling him a fat marker. "The last I knew, everyone could read."

"Yes, ma'am." He winked and followed orders. "I guess this is why Jen and Doug are hosting Thanksgiving tomorrow instead of you."

"For sure, especially with Mike calling the Riders' game in the afternoon—fortunately they're playing in town—so Jen needed to step in."

He started strolling the room, glancing at the various envelopes and printouts. "Where are the RSVPs?" he asked.

"On my computer," Lisa replied, "based on the mailed responses with payments, each table assigned and labeled. Who are you checking on?" She walked to her computer and looked at him.

"Murphy Auto Parts," he replied. "I ran into someone from the family who recognized me."

Lisa nodded without clicking the keyboard. "They bought a full table of eight, but I think they only gave me seven names." She laughed and shook her head. "I've got those whole-table reservations memorized. The Murphy's run a good business, and we like to patronize locally if possible. The grandfather and father still buy season tickets to the Riders' games and…partial season to the Red Sox." She shook her head in wonder. "I bet that's what keeps the old guy young."

Andy could think of other reasons, like an adorable baby, but kept the thought to himself.

Her eyes caught his. "Is your tuxedo pressed and ready for prime time? I'm betting our handsome eligible brother will bring in a huge hunk of change." She grinned. "We're going to have a great event and a great time."

"Maybe you will," he murmured, glancing at his watch. "Where are the kids? It's three o'clock."

"Always looking for action…"

The front door banged open and noise entered. "There's your answer," said Lisa, rising to greet her children.

"Uncle Andy's here!" shouted Briana. "Good. We're in for some fun."

Lisa's eyes shone. "That's what you're known for, little brother. It's not a bad thing. And they miss you when you're in Florida."

His winter home in Miami was what she meant.

He hugged his teenage nephew, Bobby, and leaned down to kiss Briana. "How about we mess up the kitchen and create a surprise dinner for everyone?"

"Oh, goody!" said Briana. "Those surprises turn out to be our most genius creations!" She turned to Lisa. "Mom? Are we stocked or are we bare?"

Andy was pleased Briana remembered that they used only ingredients already on hand for this cooking challenge. And by her reaction, his sister remembered, too.

Chuckling, Lisa approached Andy and wrapped her arms around him—or tried to. "Oof, you must be working out a lot. If I haven't already said it, I'm so glad to have you home for an extra while post season—even if I have to give credit to this fundraiser. And I hope you'll come back for Christmas this year."

An image of big blue eyes came into his mind, and he almost wished they hadn't. As he stepped back, however, he played it cool and simply shrugged. "Nothing's set in stone." Which was just the way he liked to live. He winked at Lisa. "Flexibility and no commitments. That's the upside to being single. A 'we'll see about Christmas' is the best I can give you."

##

Two highchairs, one booster seat… Thanksgiving at her parents' home did not resemble the idyllic greeting cards of the holiday. No quiet "please pass the butter" or "the sweet potato pie is yummy" on the lips of her family. Just voices talking over one another, increasing the decibel level with each passing minute.

Shannan sat back at the table, gazing from one family member to the other, loving each of them and happy to be ensconced, but sensing the beginning of a headache as she popped another bit of sweet potato into Maddie's mouth.

Her daughter, on the other hand, seemed to be in heaven, twisting left and right, babbling non-stop to whoever showed an interest. Which meant everyone. And wasn't that the point of moving back home? Security for her daughter, who needed loving people in her life.

Just as she did.

"Mom to Shannon...Mom to Shannon. Come in, Shannon!"

She smiled and turned to her mom. "Right here. What do you need?" She glanced at the serving dishes in front of her, ready to pass any of them down the table.

"What I need is what we all need," she said, glancing around the full table, "and that is for you to join us next week at that Delaney gala. We'd like to see you get out of the house. To be with people. And we included you when we bought a table for eight. Have you thought about it a little more?"

How odd, the quiet that settled over the room. Even the little ones had stopped their chatter.

Despite her mother's attempt, Shannon was too old to be manipulated. "And you think ganging up on me at the dinner table is the way to go?" She shook her head. "Take your foot off the gas and put your good intentions elsewhere. I'll rejoin society when I'm ready."

"And when will that be?" asked her dad, who knew how to run a business and thought he could run a family. "Matthew's gone more than three years. You're young, Shannon, and vibrant, with a long life ahead. Is waiting five years the magic number? Six? The longer you hide out, the easier it is to keep hiding. It becomes a habit."

Her parents really were ganging up on her, with a double play made more powerful by the echo of yesterday's conversation with Andy. "I'm meeting the public at the art gallery," she said. "In fact, I'm actually the best staffer to meet and greet customers. So you can all stop worrying about me. I'm not hiding."

Her sister, Amy, reached for her hand and squeezed. "I know what they say about good intentions, but we thought this gala would be perfect, since you would have us all with you." A sweet smile crossed her face. "You know—that safety in numbers thing."

Shannon's tension ebbed away. Her sister had been nothing but loyal, helpful and loving since Shannon had returned to Boston permanently over a year ago. She pressed Amy's hand, but glanced around the table until her gaze rested on her grandfather.

"No opinion, Pops? Or is discretion the better part of valor for you?" Which would have been a first for the extrovert.

Her cherished Pops's brow furrowed, and his eyes narrowed as he took in the scene before him. "Don't listen to any of 'em. My money's on you to do what you think best."

She rose and walked over to the old man, leaned down and kissed him. "I love you, Pops."

"I love you, too. And if you decide to go, you can be my date!"

CHAPTER TWO

Her cell phone rang the next morning at ten o'clock. Andy's name was on the readout. "Can you hold a sec?" she asked, tucking it under her cheek. "This child needs a bit of help in the bathroom."

"Take your time."

She was back in a minute, her eye on Maddie. "All done, so good morning. She's happily playing with puzzles and babbling away. Did you have a good turkey day?" If only that auction wasn't hanging over her head, she'd enjoy renewing the friendship.

"Couldn't get a word in edgewise at my sister's," said Andy, "so, I'd say it was a normal Delaney gathering."

"Ditto here."

"Of course," he continued, "we had one big topic of conversation with a dozen reminders of who's doing what and when and how."

The gala. "It's an awful lot of responsibility. How many guests?"

"Three hundred and fifty actual tickets sold, with other donations from folks who couldn't make it. It's our first-ever fundraiser, and I think Lisa and Mike, although a bit nervous, are pretty happy so far."

"Now all y'all have to do is pull it off."

His low chuckle was musical and upbeat. "Sounds like you brought back some Texas with you. But I guess you're right. We just need to pull off a successful party."

The question he hadn't asked yet simmered in the air around her.

"Are you and Maddie free today?" he asked, bringing her thoughts back to the present. "I've got two extra tickets on-hold at the aquarium. My nieces woke up with bellyaches and can't go."

"Sounds like too much Thanksgiving," said Shannon.

"I think you're absolutely right. So I went on-line to check out the exhibits, and the aquarium has a special kids' area for what they call an 'interactive experience.' Want to let Maddie get her hands wet?"

"Wow. Your idea came out of left field. You caught me totally by surprise."

"That's the way I like it," he replied. "And for the record, I throw from centerfield, not left. And also, for the record, I'm not going to push you about next week— so relax."

"Nice."

"As far as I'm concerned, we're two old friends, living in Boston, with an unexpected chance to catch up. So, Shannon, it's your call."

The proverbial fork in the road. Would she hide or seek? Her dad insisted her life wasn't over. Achingly, her life with Matt had ended—she glanced at her daughter—but would never be forgotten. Was there a different way forward for her? Was the time now? A first step…?

She gripped her phone tightly. "Maddie and I would love to go to the aquarium with you today. Thanks very much for the invitation."

Andy disconnected with a sigh of relief. He'd played the hand well. Once he'd ignited his memory, a lot of details emerged. She wasn't shy, just on the quiet side. With smarts and determination. When she voiced an opinion in high school, everyone on the school paper listened. She should have been the editor, but she'd loved her camera. The pictures she produced, highlighting any type story, were front-page worthy. His memories were all good, and if he could help out an old friend—a very attractive friend—to regain her footing, he'd be happy to do it. And who knew where that might lead?

He wondered about the present. Was she still passionate about photography? Had marriage, motherhood and military life put that to rest? He'd bet not.

The question about the dinner-dance would resolve itself shortly, and he'd do his bit as expected, whether she was there or not. In the meantime, he and Shannon could have a good time together. Get to know each other again. And maybe he could help her out. Seemed like a good plan for both of them.

With his current flextime, he could choose to go to Florida after the gala or hang around town for a couple of months. Until the pre-season started at the end of February, his life was his own.

Two hours later, he pulled up to the address Shannon had given him and parked in the driveway behind her car. He idly wondered why her small Toyota

17

wasn't in the garage, but forgot about it when she opened the front door after he knocked.

She looked stunning in a blue sweater that matched her eyes. And with the pink color in her cheeks… "Man, you look great."

"Thanks." She avoided his gaze, but opened the door wider. "You're always throwing me with your compliments. Guess I'm just not used to that anymore." She motioned him inside and started calling for Maddie. She didn't have to bother.

"An-dee! An-dee!" Like a miniature tornado, the child ran to him, arms up. "We see fishees now?"

"That's right, gorgeous, we're going to see some fishees," he said amid his laughter, picking her up as easily as a ground ball into his glove and shifting her to his shoulders. "You're as beautiful as your mama, and you sure like seeing the world from high up."

Andy followed her gaze as the little girl beamed at her mom. "Look at me, Mommy. High up."

But the look on Shannon's face had him concerned. "What's wrong, Shan? She seems happy."

Shannon looked from him to Maddie and slowly nodded. "Maybe I've got this all wrong," she said. "Maybe she needs to hear deep voices… No… she's got uncles and grandpas. She's not in a convent!"

She looked at up at Andy. "I'm sorry. Sometimes, I'm insecure about motherhood. I'm always questioning myself. Maybe I'm not good company today. If you want to change your mind about going…"

"Are you kidding? And break the heart of this little cutie pie?" And disappoint him as well. He carefully put Maddie down and approached the woman who seemed just a grown-up version of the girl he'd once known. Still smart, caring and determined.

"Have you forgotten, Shannon," he said quietly, "that my siblings and I had no parents at all? I was nine when they died. Jen, older. Emily was seven. Lisa and Mike had no idea how to parent us, but they never stopped trying."

Her eyes remained glued to his. Encouraged, he continued.

"So, been there, done that. I think they figured it out as they went along. And as for me…? The only thing I judge is the arc of a fly ball coming at me at Fenway Park or on the road." He let a silence punctuate his words before adding, "Understand what I'm saying?"

A smile inched its way across her face. "If I can borrow a dress and get a babysitter, I'll bid on you at the gala. You've just helped me immensely." A smile came and went. "My folks…? I love them dearly, but they worry too much. I'm under a microscope. Maybe you and I are on a level playing field. So I'd be more than happy to help you out, my non-judgmental friend."

More than her sparkling eyes and happy smile, her trust in him came through and he gulped. Trust was not a small thing! His good intentions to merely bolster her confidence suddenly seemed idiotic. Friendships between men and women usually evolved into something more or dissipated completely. He wasn't truly looking to evolve. But she wasn't another sister to him either.

"Friends do have each other's backs," he said slowly, "and although we may have time gaps, we've known each other for a long while. I'll be there for you as much as possible, Shannon." He took her hands in his. "But here's a fair warning—actually for both of us— you're a beautiful woman, and I'm a healthy, single man."

##

19

Of course, he was a man. She got that. However, he was still the upbeat and steady Andrew she once knew, and she wasn't worried about him being inappropriate.

"You're making this outing so easy," she said as Andy quickly lifted the stroller from his SUV and righted it on the sidewalk. "It takes me forever to do that."

He grunted. "I'm bigger and very experienced. Now where's Maddie?"

"Maddie's here! Pease get me out now!" came the child's voice from inside the vehicle.

Shannon chuckled as Andy's eyes widened in surprise. "She doesn't miss a thing, does she?" he asked.

"Nope," she said, reaching for her daughter. "Believe me, after a full day with her, I sleep well at night—at least since I moved back to Massachusetts last year."

"And I'd guess that's about the time she might have given up a nap?" He started walking. "And boom! You were chasing her full time."

Questions spewed forth from her. "You're single. How do you know…?

"I've got six nephews and nieces, and somehow, I'm always involved," he replied, as they began walking toward the building. "Briana was too small, born too soon, and we all held our breaths."

"Oh…"

"Not to worry. She's now eleven and plays the viola. Then Jen had the twins. And we held our breaths again. Now they're five and keep us very amused. In fact, in stitches." He laughed and shrugged. "That's how it goes. The latest rule is that we all gather for Thanksgiving in Boston. Even Brian, who lives with his family in Houston. I'm proud to say, I'm every kid's favorite uncle."

"Sounds like my family. Everyone's in everyone else's business—in a good way—mostly."

Before they reached the front doors of the aquarium, they heard the barking.

"Look, Maddie," said Shannon. "Seals! Right outside. Let's go." She glanced at Andy. "Okay with you?"

"Everything's okay. The adventure is just beginning."

An odd way to put it. She glanced at him questioningly, but he was looking ahead and pointing.

"I see an empty spot up close, right by the barrier. Let's go."

And suddenly, she was jogging to keep up with him as he pushed the stroller. Maddie was sitting forward, waving her arms, having a wonderful time and calling, "Zoom, zoom!"

"You got it." Andy picked up the pace as they ran to "their" spot.

"Look, Maddie," Shannon began. "See the seals."

The child looked around her, lifting her arms. "Up, up."

Shannon watched him scoop up her daughter and sighed comically. "I think I'm out of a job when we're together. Yay! She's getting heavy."

Maybe that's what dads were for. The heavy lifting. In many different ways. She studied the picture they made—Andrew and Maddie—and a corner of her heart tore. Matthew was missing this. Missing everything they'd dreamed about.

She took a deep breath, steadied herself. No more going backwards. That's why she'd moved home. Family support and looking ahead.

"Listen, Maddie," she said, looking up at her daughter in Andy's arms. "Can you hear the seals barking?"

Suddenly, the child's face lit up. "Doggies bark, Mommy." Without waiting for a response, the child added, "Maddie wants a doggy."

"Those are seals, Maddie. See? Seals do bark just like doggies." She paused. "Time to go inside," Shannon declared. "You can tell Grandma you saw seals today."

They opened the front doors and discovered a crowded lobby. After finding the will-call line, Shannon reached into her purse and took out her wallet.

"What are you doing?" asked Andy. "I invited you. And they're already paid for. Put that away."

"I can—"

"Nope. Not today." His voice brooked no further argument, and his normally bright green eyes changed to a dark olive color. She snapped her purse closed.

"Okay, then. Thank you."

"Atta girl."

A voice nearby called, "Hey, Andy Delaney! Resting up for the new season?"

Andy nodded. "You bet."

"Can my boy get an autograph?"

Andy glanced at Shannon. "Sorry about this." Then he waved the man over and signed his son's program. "Let's keep it between us, okay?" he asked the tween. "It's the off-season."

"You got it," said the dad. "And thanks."

They walked away with big smiles.

"Who was that autograph really for?" asked Shannon with a chuckle. "That was so cool. It reminded me that, hey...I'm with Andrew Delaney. The one and only—"

"Cut it out," he growled. "It's time to see the fish."

"Or touch the sharks and rays." She pointed at the touch-tank for kids. "You haven't changed much, Andy. Still kind of modest...not quite the show-off type as Brian was."

He studied her slowly. "That was his cover-up, Shan. His bravado. We were both trying to figure out...I don't know...maybe life itself. And now," he said, gazing down at the baby, "it's time to get on with that interactive experience. Let's take her out of the stroller."

Shannon noted his quick change of subject and agreed. But not before asking, "Have you figured out that life mystery yet? And if so, would you mind sharing? Just one hint will do."

He stepped nearer to her and stroked her cheek. "Still working on it. But as for you? You're a fighter, Shannon. Not with guns blazing, but with determination. From what I can see, you've come a long way in a short time. You're doing great."

"So good for my ego. Thank you."

While he fiddled with Maddie's safety straps, Shannon reached into the basket beneath the carriage and brought out her Nikon. She checked it over and smiled at Andy. "Now, I'm truly all set for this outing."

##

Andy glanced at what was in her hands and was struck by a thousand memories. "Now I really know I'm with Shannon Murphy!" he said. "You always had your camera with you, a regular duo."

"There were times," she said, "when a teacher would take it away, accuse me of not paying attention in class." Her eyes shone, as if keeping a secret.

"Foolish for sure," he said while lifting Maddie from the stroller, tightening his grip as she wriggled. "You were probably paying the closest attention of all."

"Just not to the subject she was teaching." The memory had put a beautiful smile on her face.

"No doubt about the subject today," he said, glancing at the child, and bringing Shannon back to

23

reality. "Snap away. Create an album. I'll keep her interested." He placed Maddie on the ground and squatted next to her. "Hold my hand, sweetie, and we can touch the special fish. Ready?"

Nodding hard, she put her hand in his, and he led the way to the tank. "Sharks, Maddie. And rays. See how flat the rays are? See their long tails?"

"Long tails."

He showed her how to make her hand flat, with palm down. "And we have to whisper," he said, demonstrating with his voice and holding a finger to his lips.

"Sh-h-h-h" she breathed, holding her own tiny finger to her mouth.

"They don't like noise."

"Ooh." She copied his hand action, and in no time, a ray was swimming under her fingers.

"Get this shot, Shannon," he called. "Look at her face!"

"Got it," said Shannon. "And more."

Two hours later, even the big shark tank couldn't hold the interest of the curious toddler.

"We are at the intersection of cranky and hungry," said Shannon, looking at her watch.

"We can fix that with some hamburgers," said Andy. He peered into the stroller. "Should we have lunch, Maddie?"

"Mom-my!" A face like a thundercloud searched for Shannon. "Time for yunch!"

"She's already eaten a sandwich, drained her thermos, devoured grapes and half a banana," Shannon said, feeling a bit defensive. "Maybe she's growing."

"That's what they tend to do," said Andy, steering the carriage to the elevator. "My sister complained about that every year when she had to buy Brian and me new clothes. We kept it simple. Same stuff, bigger sizes."

"Great idea. Simple is a wonderful goal." Too bad life had gotten terribly complicated recently.

"How do you feel about keeping it simple and finding the aquarium's café?" asked Andy. "I can use a bite, and I bet you can, too."

"Absolutely. Simple is good." Her stomach growled just then, bringing them both to laughter. She'd refuse him almost nothing for the wonderful day Maddie and she were enjoying. Impetuously, she squeezed his arm.

"Thanks so much, Andy. I'm having a great time today. Such fun. You may have grown up, but you haven't changed on the inside. I liked you then, and I like you now. I think Lisa and Mike...?" She smiled at him. "They figured out how to keep you all going and-and-at least not make it worse."

Her gaze went to Maddie. "I pray I can emulate them. She's...she's..."

Andy's hand found hers. "She's in good hands. You're the same person inside, too, Shan. Lousy experiences leave scars, but we adjust. We figure it out as we go along because we have no choice. Not if we want to grab some happiness."

"Man, you sound like a philosopher," Shannon said, spotting a table and pointing.

"Ha! Not usually, and never out loud, except maybe with my brother. But I was only a kid and have had a long time to think about stuff." He paused, and she felt the weight of his gaze on her. "For you, it's not as long. But you're trying. That's what counts. I know you'll get there."

He didn't know how hard each decision was for her, how shaky the tightrope she walked with her in-laws, how she had to budget every penny from her monthly income. Army pensions were not huge. She loved her part-time job at the art gallery, but much of her salary went toward daycare.

"Thanks for your vote of confidence. Sometimes, I need one."

"Isn't that what friends are for?" he asked, the warmth of his smile reflecting the warmth in his voice. A very soothing combination.

CHAPTER THREE

Despite recomputing her budget to include a new dress, Shannon expected the harder item to cross off her to-do list was asking Matthew's parents to babysit on the night of the gala. Not that they didn't want to see Maddie. In fact, they wanted to see her every day! The situation had become dicey when Shannon opted to live near her own family, rather than in Amherst, the college town where Matthew's family still resided. A two-hour road trip between them seemed reasonable to her, and certainly not a hardship to the end of the world.

Perhaps her in-laws' deep grief had affected their judgment, considering Matt had been their only child. Shannon understood that. She'd mourned for them as well as for herself. But despite their many entreaties, she had quietly stuck to her own plans.

With her cell phone in hand the next morning, she pressed their number and hoped for the best.

27

"Shannon? Is that you?" asked her mother-in-law. "You didn't call on Thanksgiving. Maybe you were too busy with your family?"

Oh, boy. Not a great beginning. "Susan, I left a message on your new cell phone. Do you know how to retrieve messages?" The woman wasn't old, just old-fashioned and set in her ways. Last month, however, she'd decided to "break out of her rut" and bought the latest in mobile phones so "she wouldn't miss any calls." Except she had.

"I have a happy reason for calling," Shannon began. "How'd you like to babysit overnight? It's been a few weeks since our last visit." When she finished explaining about the gala, silence met her ears for a moment.

"Of course, we'd love to babysit," Susan said, "but could you explain this again. You're going to a big party?"

"It's dinner-dance for a children's charity, Susan. It's at a hotel, and my family bought a whole table to support the cause." She left out the part about the auction.

"Oh. A family thing. But with music and dancing." There was silence for a moment. Then Shannon heard a sigh. "Well, it's been three years since...since Matt... I guess you're at the point where you want to start over. Maybe dance with someone else."

Oh, God. Susan's voice...almost cracking. "No one's forgetting Matt," said Shannon, her own voice quivering. "He'll always be part of me. And he's definitely Madison's daddy." She took a breath. "Frankly, I'm a little nervous, myself, Susan. I've never enjoyed large gatherings, but at least I'll have support at this one."

"I guess you made the right decision when you came back," said Susan, "but...please just don't forget about us here in Amherst."

Shannon blinked hard. "How can I forget Maddie's grandma and grandpa? The more family, the better. You're both too important."

Her mother-in-law chuckled. "You're a good girl, Shannon. It's just that..."

"I know...we all have our moments. And we handle them as best we can."

She disconnected after solidifying arrangements and laid her head on her arms. Everything was so hard. What a crash from the high she'd felt yesterday with Andy. A sweet day. A special time-out-of-time for her. A taste of normalcy.

Susan's words stayed with her—something about starting over and dancing with someone else...

She wasn't sure about the first part. But the image of a well-built baseball player with a pair of green eyes shimmied in her mind. Yeah. She could picture a dance.

##

Her own mother was impossible, too, just in a different way. An hour after hanging up with Susan, the phone rang. Her upbeat mom was full of new reasons for Shannon to join them at the gala.

"Hold up, Mom. Now that I have reliable sitters, I've decided to go. Happy now?"

"Wow! Was that all that really stopped you? I'm so relieved."

Her mom viewed the world with a glass always half-full, which made her a wonderful mother when raising young children. She was always ready with solutions to their problems, and had energy for fun outings, whether to the neighborhood library or for a rare skiing weekend. Helen focused on practical fixes and tended to put emotional adjustments aside with the phrase, "it's just a stage. You'll get over it."

Shannon's situation had rocked her. But true to form, Helen's feistiness was still on display.

"You said sitters?" her mom asked. "Plural? Have you met some nice teenage girls in your neighborhood? That would be great."

An idea for another time—no more ignoring the need. "Better than teens, Mom. Susan and John are driving in."

A moment of silence from Helen. Shannon could sense her mom digesting this new information.

"Wow. Susan and John?" asked Helen. "That's a surprise. Well, good for them."

"I agree. It's all good. Maddie will be well taken care of, and I won't worry."

"That's settled then, so on to the next item," said Helen. "Since you're joining us at the party, it's time to go shopping for a new dress. Our treat—your dad insists."

"Bringing in the big guns, huh? But the answer's no. I plan on visiting consignment shops where the price is right, and the clothing can be fabulous, too."

"Then I'll join you," insisted Helen. "Can't we just have a fun day together? Shopping, lunching? Stealing some mother-daughter time...I want to become reacquainted with my wonderful daughter again."

Shannon squeezed her eyes shut. Matt's death had reverberated in so many ways. It seemed everyone wanted a piece of her. Everyone was struggling to adjust.

"Your daughter is trying to find herself, Mom. I love you, too."

"Good. I'm picking you up in an hour. Maddie needs a girl's day out!"

##

She texted Andy before her mom came.

Progress. Have babysitters. Looking for dress. Wonderful time yesterday. Thanks again.

His reply came almost instantly.

Atta girl! Knew I could count on u. Don't sweat the dress. Call u later.

Shannon had never actually experienced the term "shop til you drop" until that afternoon with her mom. Wrong color, wrong design, or out-of-style. She'd compiled a list of places and drove to each one, taking Maddie in and out of the car. By late afternoon, she'd resigned herself to visiting a department store during the week. Until they walked into the very last shop on the list. And saw *the* dress.

A rich, blue-gray color, beaded, and in a tea length with short sleeves and a jewel neckline. Also her size, and it fit perfectly on her five-foot five-inch frame.

"It's a winner," said Helen. "The color, the style and fit. You look gorgeous."

Shannon gazed at herself in the dressing room mirror. "It's classic. Not too revealing, but still…um…flattering." She'd been about to say tantalizing or sexy, but changed her word choice at the last minute. *Sexy* was not on her agenda.

"Yes, this will do it." She took it off and handed it to her mom while she got dressed. "For once, I didn't check the price before trying on. Can you please find the tag and let me know the damage."

But she was talking to Helen's back. "Too low to mention," called her mom. "I'm taking care of it. Go find shoes."

Shannon sighed and looked at her daughter, playing on the floor. "Your grandma is impossible, Maddie. You know that?"

Maddie's blue eyes met her own before looking about. "Grandma? Dere's Grandma," she said, pointing at the woman.

Shannon scooped her up from the floor where she'd been—holy moly—playing with straight pins. "You love grandma, don't you? And grandma and I love you!" She bestowed kisses on her child all over her face and neck, then gave her a raspberry.

Maddie's laughter always set her world aright. What a delicious baby! She'd do anything for her daughter. Anything at all. Walking out of the dressing room, she spotted her mom at the cash register. Yeah, Shannon would even insist on buying Maddie a second-hand dress if necessary. Brand new, too.

Oh-h- and ouch. She hadn't allowed her own mom the same privilege. Money seemed to be her sore point.

"I'll look for shoes during the week," she said as they left the shop. "Thanks a lot for the dress, Mom. I really appreciate it."

"My pleasure," said Helen. "Money should be the least of your problems. Dad and I worked hard to grow the business. Now your brother is bringing in his ideas and doing the same. Fortunately, we're doing well. We can help you without hurting ourselves, if that's what you're concerned about."

Her folks' security hadn't crossed her mind. She would have known if Murphy's Auto Parts was in trouble.

"I'm very glad to hear it, and I love you all," Shannon said, trying to choose her words carefully. "But please understand that Matt and I took pride in standing on our own two feet. And even though Matt's gone now, I intend to continue that way. I'm not your little girl who still needs to be taken care of, Mom. You know that, right?" She opened the car door and watched Maddie climb into her special seat. "But it's good to know you're in the background if needed." She gave her mom a kiss on the cheek. "I'm really grateful for you being there."

Helen wrapped her around and hugged tight. "You're still my baby. Nothing's too much. Hear me? Nothing."

"Then how about being my back-up Maddie sitter? *That* would ease my mind regarding extra work hours, especially during the holiday season. In fact, if you can take her tomorrow, I'll call in and say I'm available. Sunday at the shop is always busy now, and I know the manager will grab me."

Helen grinned. "What a terrible ask." She got into the car and turned her head. "Hey, Maddie. You wanna play with Grandma tomorrow?"

As Shannon watched the interplay, her heart melted at the love she saw between generations. Maddie and she both needed the love of home. As for the other grandparents…she truly hoped they'd support her stepping into the wider world and continue to be part of the family circle.

Maddie went down for the night a little past seven. Shannon turned on the baby monitor in her daughter's room and brought the matching monitor to the basement with her. Unlike in Texas, most New England homes had the advantage of basements, useful for many things and a big selling point for Shannon when purchasing her small house.

She'd finally have her own darkroom again. Although she took many digital pictures—who didn't, with the latest in cell phone options? —her greatest joy with photography came from working with film. Old school, perhaps, but she was not alone in the belief that film provided more substance and depth, much more nuance in the finished product. An almost tactile experience. The excitement of watching a photograph come slowly to life and being able to adjust the image never failed to fascinate and challenge her.

The Nikon she'd used at the aquarium the day before was her go-to film camera. And now she was eager to start the development process.

She'd set the darkroom up in a far corner, away from the stairs, away from the laundry area, away from any place that might attract a toddler. With her camera in one hand and a flashlight in the other, she made her way to the work area, then turned off the flashlight. Color film, sensitive to all parts of the visual spectrum, had to be handled in complete darkness.

With practiced hands, she removed the film, unrolled and wound it on the attached reel, then placed it in the film tank. She covered the tank and turned the flashlight back on. Now she could light the overheads as well.

Time passed quickly as she continued the developing process in the tank, adding developer and water, gently shaking, pouring out and adding fixer. It was a specific process using a timer for each step of the way.

At the end of her session, she hung up the film to dry. Later on, she'd cut the film into strips of negatives and begin printing. That's when she'd discover if she'd captured any magic.

As if by design, her cell phone rang as she reentered her kitchen. She smiled when she spotted Andy's name.

"Hi, Andy. Was your day as productive as mine?"

His chuckle kept the smile on her face. "You don't want to go there. Now I think the entire Delaney family would like this great event to be over. Too many phone calls, too many changes, tables, decorations, music. Normally, my sister would be an asset to the army, except now she's ready for a breakdown."

"Sorry about that. The military's entire *modus operandi* is organization- based. Every procedure or event is pre-planned and figured out beforehand. Maybe you could create a manual now as a reference for next year. Or you could use a party planner, and have less stress. Maybe next time…?"

Andy's laughter was contagious. "Nothing's changed, Shannon. You're still a problem-solver. Still smart as ever. I always admired that about you."

She wouldn't have guessed his opinion of her at all in the three years they'd overlapped in high school. He and Brian had been part of the elite group. Baseball stars. Good grades. Handsome. With an older brother-in-law who was an NFL quarterback for the hometown Riders. Those twins had it made socially. Why would he ever think about an everyday sort like her?

"I had no idea you felt that way," she said. "The teenage Andy wasn't truly shy, so he must have kept his personal thoughts to himself on purpose."

"The teenage Andy barely knew up from down or east from west," said the man in question. "He was trying to figure out a hell of a lot of stuff. Whatever made sense came out in writing. In fact, it still does." He paused for a moment before he said, "Nowadays, I write a monthly blog called *Beyond the Locker Room*. Believe it or not, I actually have more than a million followers. But back then, my English teachers loved me."

"Wow! That's impressive. So working on the paper was a natural fit. Your columns were always great."

"Writing helped. My dad—he played ball with us. My mom—she loved stories. They both loved music. I just wanted…oh, forget it. How'd we get on this topic anyway? Oh, right. Problem-solving for the gala."

She let him change the topic, but a frisson of anxiety ran through her. Memories of his parents traveled with him back then—in class, at the newspaper, on the baseball field. Memories still traveled with him. Just like her memories of Matt lingered. But little Maddie would have no memories of a father she hadn't known. Shannon had thought about that many times, aiming to bring Matt to life for his daughter through pictures and stories. As soon as she could understand.

"Someone actually mentioned a party planner," said Andy, "but oh, no. It would be a waste of money—funds that could go to the kids."

His words brought her back to the present. "Not a job for a volunteer, huh?"

"Probably not. Just remember, you're my personal volunteer, and your job is to bid."

"Right. Here's my question—it will be a big crowd, with the single women keeping an eye on the bachelors. What if you get lots of admirers? It's your money. How high should my bid go?"

"Over the top, Shan, right over the top. Haven't I mentioned that?"

She couldn't imagine the amount of that final bid. In her mind, Andrew Delaney, with his charm, good looks and talent, would be the catch of the night. But no one else would have an inkling of the intellectual and emotional depth inside the man.

"Over the top? If you say so…"

"I do say so. Think of it this way – after you win, you'll be going on your first date, getting your feet wet, so to speak. And you'll be comfortable with me while I enjoy myself immensely, too. Remember, you're saving me. You can even pick the place and time. I'd also be happy to drive you home after the gala."

"Uh…that last one's not a great idea." But everything else he said made sense. Except…he didn't need saving. With his social skills, she knew he could handle any high bidder.

"Is something wrong?" Andy asked. "I drink in moderation if that's what's worrying you."

"Never crossed my mind," she replied. "It's the babysitters."

"Huh?"

"Maddie's other grandparents. So…." She let her voice trail off.

Silence met her ear for a moment. "I see," he said slowly, thoughtfully. "Then I'll definitely take a raincheck on that drive."

He did understand. She could sense he picked up on the emotional landmine. But he hadn't backed off entirely. Shannon suspected that raincheck would be put to use. The boy she remembered had become a man— quite an impressive one. Smart, caring and funny with sex appeal to spare. If she were being honest with herself, she'd admit that. From his wavy brown hair to his broad shoulders and strong arms.

Humming a popular, upbeat tune, she prepared for bed with Andy Delaney on her mind. As she pulled down the covers, she waited a moment, taking stock. Not a shred of guilt wafted through her. Of course, she'd made no promises or commitments either, other than going to that gala.

She picked up the framed photo of her husband that sat on her end table and stroked the glass. "I'm going to tuck our love into a corner of my heart, Matt. I'll bring you to life for Maddie with stories and pictures. I promise you'll never be forgotten. That would be impossible." She blinked back tears and carefully replaced the photo on the table.

Perhaps Andrew Delaney would be the next chapter in her life. Perhaps only a friendly stepping-stone to the future. She didn't know. But her clear conscience convinced her she was moving in the right direction.

CHAPTER FOUR

As soon as Shannon entered the Greenburg Gallery
where she worked, the manager, Heather Greenburg,
rushed over to greet her.

"Thank goodness you're here today, and a little
early, too," Heather said, smiling and ushering her in.
"The good news is that we've had a lot of foot traffic
over the weekend. The bad news is that my mom's in a
tizzy about leaving the front of the shop unmanned while
we're on the floor with customers." She raised her eyes
to the second level of the gallery. "Yesterday was a
madhouse, but now that you're here, Mom will calm
down. We've also decided to add a college intern to the
staff—an art major."

"Great idea. And I'll be in every day this week
through Friday," promised Shannon, taking off her
jacket. She caught Heather's eye. "I'm really sorry, but
next weekend won't work for me. I will reserve the

Sundays afterwards, though. Remember, I mentioned weekend issues at the beginning?"

"Yes, yes, but that was six months ago, during the summer," replied Heather. "Time's sped by. If the intern doesn't start this week, I'll just have to drag my daughter in next Saturday. You can imagine a twelve-year-old has absolutely no interest in being here." Shrugging, Heather sighed. "I guess, as they say, it is what it is."

They walked to a private office in the rear, where Shannon left her jacket and purse, but she took her cell phone with her as she made her way back up front, perusing the hanging art and reminding herself about the details she'd need to know if asked, until she stopped cold in front of a framed photo with a sold sign on it. It rested on a lone easel where the wall angled into the room. She started to shake and felt beads of perspiration popping all over herself.

"Heather!"

"Surprise, Shannon!" It was Lynn's voice. Heather's mom. "Your picture sold. I knew it would! As a matter of fact, we've had several inquiries. But all you needed was the right match."

Kind of like a marriage. The random thought zigzagged through her stunned mind.

Ordinarily, it would have taken years of submissions for her work to be displayed in a Newbury Street gallery. She'd been slowly building a portfolio of her best photographs and had also been the photographer for unofficial events on the army base. She'd had some success when showing her work professionally in Texas—a few bank lobbies, a community art display, a hospital gallery. And the sales she'd made there had encouraged her.

But with so much distraction and grief after Matt's death, submitting to Boston galleries hadn't occurred to her. She'd been fully engaged in her relocation, caring for an infant and job hunting.

The Greenburg ladies, however, both experts in the world of commercial art, had warmly embraced her as their assistant, encouraging her to grow a career. A person like Shannon should be managing a gallery, they seemed to think. Aware of the Nikon always at her side, they'd insisted on seeing her work, and afterwards immediately allocated her a spot on that easel for the holiday season. And here she was, blown away by her latest sale.

The women embraced her, congratulated her. The piece, called *Wisdom,* had been on display for only a week.

"And it's being picked up today," said Lynn.

Heather confirmed her mom's words. "You'll never guess who bought it," she added, not waiting for an answer. "Retired quarterback, Mike Brennan. He popped in here on a whim two days ago on his way to the airport—I think Christmas gifts were on his mind—and never stepped past your photo."

"Really? That's something." She sounded like an idiot, but how strange that Andy's brother-in-law happened to connect with the gallery where she worked. Oh, well. Boston wasn't The Big Apple. More like an apple fritter.

"He said it was perfect for his wife. Special. Paid for it right then and there, but couldn't take it with him."

"Not to the airport, but maybe it's also a surprise," murmured Shannon, studying the work and trying to understand the quarterback's vision. What had he seen in it?

She'd used sepia tones to wash over a black and white print. Moonlight revealed a wide-eyed barn owl perched near the top of the loft. His wings were slightly spread. Behind him, sitting on a bale of hay, was a little girl wearing oversized glasses and reading a book—with a flashlight. Both the owl and the child had dark eyes and heart-shaped faces. Shannon had slightly colorized the child's clothing to match the owl's rusty-orange back feathers.

Her darkroom allowed this creativity. Using film for the setting and digital photography with the child allowed it too. Her imagination had fueled the result. "Did Mr. Brennan say anything about it?" she asked, waving at the print.

"That it looked as if the owl was protecting the child," said Heather.

Shannon's hand fisted over her heart. "Exactly," she whispered. "Passing down wisdom with care and love." As she was desperately trying to do for Maddie.

"Which was why Brennan said it was perfect for his wife," Heather added.

Shannon mentally replayed everything Andy had mentioned about his family and understanding took root. Mike Brennan not only loved his wife but knew her well.

Points for the Brennan/Delaney family.

And dollars for her own pocket.

Andy waited until five o'clock to stop by the gallery for his brother-in-law's picture. Not that he wouldn't have called Shannon anyway to enjoy a quick dinner with Maddie on a Sunday evening. Maybe watch that night's Riders game together. His whole family had gathered at Jen and Doug's during the afternoon. When he left to get the picture, he'd promised to call them. But that was all he'd promised. Didn't say he'd return.

"Very mysterious these days is my bro," joked Brian, with a quick look of inquiry.

"All is well," Andy replied. Some things were better not shared too quickly. Easier to avoid questions.

Now, as he opened the door to the gallery, his eyes lit up at seeing Shannon. She'd risen immediately, probably thinking he was another customer to wait on.

"Andy!" she said. "You're the pick-up! How nice."

The thing about blondes was that their coloring gave them away. A rosy neck, a rosy face—she was embarrassed, but the warmth of her greeting had been real.

He walked over and automatically hugged her, enjoyed how she leaned against him. "It feels like a long time…"

"Two days…with a phone call yesterday."

He liked the fact she was keeping tabs. Unusual for him, who preferred to keep relationships with women light. His thoughts confused him, but one thing he knew for sure—she was a refreshing change from the groupies that hung around the hotels when he was on the road. Shannon was also a change from the relaxed social life he had in Florida during the off-season. His plane ticket to the sunshine state was confirmed for a week after the gala. He'd bought it w-a-y in advance. Couldn't take a chance of being shut out during the holidays.

"I can give you a tour if you'd like," Shannon offered, just as the front door opened again. "Sorry. Do you want to wait, or should I get Heather to wrap the picture for you?"

"Easy decision, Shan. I'll browse while you work."

Her smile reached those beautiful eyes. "Love my work, especially today." She gave him a small wave and headed to the new gallery visitors.

He'd ask her later what she meant. Now he began strolling, then pausing. Peering. Backing up. Nodding. Cocking his head.

"You look like you're having many conversations with yourself," said a woman wearing an ID tag—Heather. The co-worker Shannon had just alluded to.

"Shannon mentioned your name," he said, extending his hand. "Andy Delaney."

"I know," she said, clasping it. "I'm a big Sox fan—like the rest of Boston. So, you're a friend of Shannon's?" Her eyes narrowed slightly, as if sizing him up, and he felt the atmosphere cool.

"We go back a long time," he replied, leaving her to wonder. He waved at the displays. "It's really up close and personal in here. Not like at a museum."

The air between them warmed slightly. "Clever to change the subject, but just to let you know—Shannon's special to us. She's knows her stuff and we're crazy about her. She's got friends here."

"Shannon makes friends wherever she goes," he said nonchalantly.

She gave him a once-over, seemed to come to a conclusion, and nodded.

"Okay, then. You seem to be enjoying the art. I'll ask her give you a tour. You'll learn plenty."

"I'm sure I would, but she's got a customer."

He sensed Heather's change of attitude even before she winked at him. Business before pleasure. "Not a problem. I'll take over."

Whew! She sure tried to do exactly that. But Heather left his mind as soon as Shannon approached. "Ready for your tour? And then I'll wrap Mike's gift."

There was something about how she said it, a kind of suppressed excitement. As an actress, she'd flunk.

"What's going on, Shan? You look like you're ready to burst."

"I am! Come with me." She took his arm, led him back around to the front of the store and pointed to a picture resting on an easel. "This is the one Mike bought."

"Funny," he said, "It caught my eye right away, as soon as I left you to go browse." Noticing details played a big part of his life. His career demanded it—and he hit the mark now, too, as he noted the signature in the lower right-hand corner. *Shannon.*

Pride swelled inside him. He pivoted toward her, sensing his mouth turning into a jack-o-lantern grin. "You! It's yours. Wow. Congratulations. It's a terrific piece. I can understand why Mike wanted it," he said more slowly, as he studied the subject matter. "A familiar sensibility...Lisa, the wise one, looking out for the child. She's raised a number of us...some difficult years."

Her eyes shone; she was blinking hard. Her picture had made his own heart pang, but, uh-oh. Tears? Couldn't have that.

"I'd start dancing you around the place, but we'd break a few things. Can we go out to celebrate instead— after we package this precious artwork?"

She stepped toward him, reached for his arm and squeezed. "It's okay, Andy. Not going to drench you," she said. "But you know how it is during a game, when you walk to the plate, eye that perfect pitch and hit the ball out of the park?"

He'd been there, done that. "Absolutely. That's when I trot around the bases, waving to the fans and hearing them cheer. It's fantastic."

"Well, that's how I feel now. I worked on this picture a while ago. My sense of it—my intuition—got my hopes up. But I didn't know how others would see it."

"But now you know."

"Now I've hit it out of the park!"

A perfect topic for *Beyond the Locker Room*. Everyone has a chance to hit it out of the park. "Absolutely. I knew you would—way back then." He crossed his arms in front of his chest, changed his voice to an older-and-wiser tone, and said, "Young lady, you are living up to your potential. Keep up the good work!"

He had her laughing as they brought the piece into the back workshop for packaging. "He's going to let Lisa frame it. He didn't want the responsibility."

"Smart man," said Shannon.

"I'd love to take you dinner, Shannon. It's a special day."

He saw her answer before she spoke. "Maddie's with my folks, and that's where I'm going now. If I don't get her to sleep by seven-thirty, she'll be a witch tomorrow. I don't want bad reports from the daycare."

"Then how about I meet you back at your house with some takeout? Italian? Chinese? What do you like?" Man, what was up with him? Why was he pushing this? "C'mon. We need to celebrate."

Her smile—beautiful. Sweet. He wanted to kiss that mouth.

"Thanks, Andy. It sounds good, but do you have time? Seems like your family is keeping you running."

"Multi-tasking is my specialty. So, what's your pleasure?"

"Let's keep it simple. How about a pizza? With pepperoni? Maybe mushrooms?"

She seemed totally relaxed and happy with his idea. "Any way you want it," he said. "I know a place..."

"Everybody knows a place, but please—don't go all the way to The North End. I'm too hungry to wait!"

##

As per her text, she'd left the front door unlocked for him—not something he'd ever advise. Stepping over the threshold, he heard the sounds of Shannon putting Maddie to sleep. The bedrooms were in the back of the house, but the love words between mama and her baby traveled. *Definitely a package deal.*

His stomach tightened suddenly as the scope of the last five days hit him. A widow. A child. Her in-laws. He and Shannon hadn't seen each other in what? About thirteen or fourteen years. They weren't teens anymore, and this wasn't one of his brother-in-law Doug's Broadway plays. Genuine reality was happening in this house. Complicated real life.

Unlike his own. Sure, he kept up with family and certainly stayed on top of his career, but mostly, he lived worry-free. Intentionally. Until recently, when he'd begun feeling a little uneasy. Maybe age was catching him by surprise. Lots of friends were pairing up, getting married, including his own brother.

Brian had endured some slings and arrows during his romance with Megan Ross, but in the end? A perfect match. "If she's not worth fighting for, then she's not the one," he'd said to Andy.

Andy agreed, but also realized his own life would change, too, from that moment. He and Brian would always be tight, but his brother had fallen in love and moved forward. He'd taken on a wife and new son. A new family. Being a third wheel was not Andy's style.

As he laid the pizza on the table, waves of other memories rolled over him, bringing him back to the black time, the time when his best friend, other than Brian, was a notebook. To the time when the nine-year-old twins shared one bedroom, scared, sad and dependent on each other to get by. Hiding emotional stuff from Lisa. Looking to Mike for hints on how to get through the days. How to "man-up."

In retrospect, he now saw that Mike, himself, had been "manning-up." Or trying to. The guy had only been twenty-three when he'd taken all of them on!

He heard light footsteps and Shannon appeared, her welcoming smile chasing his dark thoughts away.

"Wonderful timing, Andy. She's down and out…thank goodness, but if we have a leftover slice, it will be her lunch tomorrow. Her favorite finger food." She peeped up at him. "Bad mommy. Too spicy. But she loves it."

"Fantastic mommy. Don't you doubt it. That is one happy kiddo." He dipped into his take-out bag of pizza accessories and produced paper plates and napkins. "No dishes for the successful photographer. And," he said with a flourish, "bring out the glasses. I found a package store and got some champagne."

Her eyes widened. A smile formed. "So-so thoughtful. Andy, you are too much! But in a very good way," she amended, reaching into her cabinet for the glasses. "When I picked Maddie up, my mom and dad wanted to celebrate, too." She turned her head toward him. "I was so excited, I had to tell them. But I wanted to get back here."

"Well…you wanted to get Maddie to sleep, right?"

She hesitated as she rejoined him at the table. "That was one reason." Her gaze met his. "Since we bumped into each other last week, Andy, I've been a bit happier. I've started to understand how my social life needs to grow again. Family is great and all that…but people also need—at least, *I* need—to widen my circle. Find some good friends. So, thank you for reminding me."

He'd had no clear motivation after they'd initially met up other than to be supportive, friendly. Seemed he'd succeeded in making her move to Boston "happier." And that was great. "No thanks needed. Glad

I could help. Now, eat up before this delectable meal grows cold."

They both dug in, drank some champagne and played the "do you remember game" along with the "whatever happened to" game. Only a small number of friends actually overlapped. And neither of them had ever used social media to find the answers.

"I guess working on the school paper was our biggest common denominator," said Shannon. "And I also guess we've really been focused on our own lives." She gathered the paper goods and disposed of them. "Of course, everyone knows what happened to you and Brian! At least, professionally." She leaned against the sink. "So tell me the truth, Andrew, how does it feel to be famous?"

He could see the laughter in her eyes and knew she was teasing. Sitting back in his chair, he wondered whether to play along like a publicity hound or give her the real story. He decided on the latter.

"I feel like a regular guy. I try not to brag, show off or name-drop."

"Huh? That doesn't sound like a prescription for fame."

"House rules—and my rules—for being famous. Kids who dream of going pro read my stuff, and I want them to know how important it is to be a regular guy—or girl—too. That's how we were raised. And if we wanted to stay in Mike's good graces, we followed orders. Which is why I can say that while I try not to disappoint the fans, I don't feel particularly famous."

"That's...that's unbelievable."

He raised his hand. "Don't get me wrong. I love the game. Always have. Nothing beats hearing the crack of my bat against a hard-pitched ball or making an 'impossible' catch in centerfield. When I hear the crowd roar, I'm happy. And I know I'm doing my job."

She didn't respond for at least thirty seconds. No flip answers, not even gentle teasing. Her brow creased. Her eyes, those lovely eyes she used for taking top-flight pictures, moved slowly over him, like an MRI scanning him inside. What did she see? What could she see?

Her hand reached out, and he encased it with his own. "Come with me," she said with a lightness in her voice. "I want to show you my etchings—sort of!"

He burst out laughing and followed her to the basement.

CHAPTER FIVE

She turned on the lights at the top of the stairs and led him to her darkroom.

"I've already created the negatives from the roll of film," she said. "So now we turn them into contact prints, which are small versions of the photos, so we can see which ones we want to enlarge—if any. I'm nothing if not practical. This is a good cost-saving measure."

She stepped in front of him and began to assemble the fixer, developer, stop bath, water, the important photographic paper and the enlarger.

"What are on those negatives?" Andy asked.

"Oh…you'll recognize the scenes. Lots of sea creatures." Most shots would probably be fine, but she really hoped for a couple of winners.

"Right. You were very busy with your camera that day."

"You were, too, with your phone, if I remember correctly."

"The difference between us, Shannon, is…umm…I can't guarantee results!'

Soon her strips of negatives revealed the pictures, each exactly the same size. She held up the sheet and began to examine them. "We can get rid of this one and that one… "She turned to him. "See how I heartless I am?"

"You are! I think they're all good. I think you're very, very good using that little toy."

"Andy—dude," she joked, "you're great for my ego, but it's either a home run or it isn't. Thanks, anyway." She put the work aside and turned back toward him.

He stepped closer and drew her gently into his arms. "Sometimes," he said, his voice husky, "a base hit wins the game." His green eyes were almost black, his lids half-way down, his mouth moving closer. His arms tightened around her slightly before the pressure stopped, and he waited.

Perhaps she'd been waiting, too. She stroked his cheek, trailed a finger over his well-defined lips and rose to her tiptoes.

That's all it took. His embrace tightened, his mouth covered hers, the kiss gentle—at first—and then demanding. She met his hunger with equal force, enjoying the contact, but then—almost in shock— stepped back, her breath catching with irregular gasps. She heard Andy exhale, too, but he stood totally still, again waiting for her.

"I-I'm sorry," she said. "You're not Matt…but…"

"I've wanted to do that all night…."

"I surprised myself—in a good way. I thought I was ready for something like this, but I didn't know how ready I was," she said.

First, his killer smile, then his laughter rang out, and she joined him in it. She touched his arm, and he pulled her close. "Regardless of my discovery," she said, "I need a little time. I'm still putting it all together."

He nodded. "I hear you. Take all the time you need. Believe it or not, Shan, I've shocked myself, too. This isn't my usual…umm…M.O., shall we say."

She wasn't worried. He'd proven his kindness and she trusted him. Besides, time had a way of being elastic. When life was bad, a day lasted for years; when life was good, a day flew by in a minute. She'd already experienced the whole gamut and noted that the time she'd spent with Andy had wings.

She chose to enlarge eight prints of the twenty-four. "This one I'll frame for my in-laws as a gift," she said, indicating one of Maddie in her stroller, her face alight and her arms up, as if saying, "get me outta here!"

"Good one," Andy said. "You caught her exactly right. It tells a little story, shows some emotion."

"Thanks." More important, Andy wasn't in this shot. Safe for grandma and grandpa.

Of the remaining prints, there was one that grabbed her in the gut. Perhaps a money-shot.

"Before I get too excited," she said, forcing herself to speak calmly, "and because I think you have a pretty good eye, I'll ask you a question." She took a breath. "Does any one picture of these seven stand out to you?"

His gaze rested on her before attending to the choices. She watched him study each photo. Saw him go back a second time, then a third to her money-shot.

No faces. Two hands—one small and one large one—next to each other in the aquarium's touch tank, with the rays swimming exactly beneath them. Perfect timing! The fingers of the man's other hand could be detected around the child's waist. Soft light reflected on the water, enhancing the scene beneath the surface.

"I can soften the other visitors so they become background," she murmured, "leaving the spotlight on yours and Maddie's hands." She twirled to him. "It's good, isn't it? Or am I being silly?"

"It's more than good," Andy said. "They could be anyone's hands. It packs an emotional wallop, and the universal message really gets you right here." He patted his chest to imitate a beating heart. Then his head tilted as he continued to look. "There's a story here, too, just like in the picture Mike bought. Simply different stories. Right?"

"Exactly the point," she said, again delighted with his insight. "Viewers can relate to their own families, to that parent and child relationship. Protection and love." She took a breath. "It's about being human. Striking that chord. Maybe, just maybe, when it's ready, I can display this one in the shop, too."

He leaned over and kissed her. "No need for that. I'd like to buy it myself."

Out of left field. Or centerfield. "No way, Andrew."

Oh, his expression! Shocked. Didn't he realize he'd given her so much already, something that couldn't be measured in dollars? She tilted her head back and met his gaze. "It's yours when I'm finished. As a gift."

She saw his immediate reaction and held up her hand. "That's the deal, Andy. Please—don't deny me the pleasure."

He said nothing, but the warmth in his eyes heated up a notch, a slow, tender smile appeared, and then he pulled her close and kissed her again.

This time, she didn't pull away.

##

Her in-laws showed up exactly at noon the following Saturday, a bit anxious, but in good spirits. Shannon had prepared lunch, but their attention was fully on Maddie. The little imp could charm the birds out of the trees, and she charmed Matt's parents, who now didn't have time to ask Shannon any questions. A good arrangement for a while, until Maddie needed her nap.

"Not so delightful now," joked Shannon, lifting her cranky daughter and heading for Maddie's bedroom. She turned her head. "Give her an hour or so, and she'll be fine again."

"I know about children," said Susan. "I raised one, you know."

The comment carried an underlying message, which Shannon ignored as she closed Maddie's door and coaxed her daughter to sleep. A song, a story—in as boring a voice as she could produce. Within ten minutes, Maddie was out, and Shannon stepped into her own bedroom to grab an extra pillow, sheet and blanket to use later after the dinner-dance.

"Hello again." Shannon placed the bedding at the end of the sofa. "I'll sleep here tonight, of course, while you take my room. Everything's clean. And if I haven't said it before, I really appreciate you coming today." She smiled at them, and said, "I wouldn't leave Maddie with just anybody, you know." Now, if that didn't make them feel special, she didn't know what else to say.

"She's a darling girl," said Susan. "In fact, John and I were wondering if one of these weekends, Maddie could visit us at our house. We've already picked out a bedroom for her. Right across from Matt's. We could paint it pink and..."

The woman was running away with herself and her ideas. John glanced at Shannon and immediately patted his wife's hand. "Hold on there, honey. You caught Shannon by surprise. One step at a time. Remember?"

So, was this a plan they'd both concocted? She had to set them straight—in a nice way. Shannon pulled a dining room chair over and sat down opposite the couple. "If I remember correctly, Maddie and I are spending Christmas Day with you this year--which is at the end of the month. Right?"

Susan nodded.

"So, that's pretty soon. We'll find other weekends for you to come over, so don't worry. We'll have regular visits."

"Except for her blue eyes, she looks just like Matt," whispered Susan. "Dark hair, the brow, the jawline. How she moves."

Now Shannon started to be concerned. Helen was off the mark. "Her hair is almost as dark. I'll give you that. But she's a real combination. Unique. Like most children are."

Susan's eyes filled, and Shannon backed off. "You know what they say about beauty being in the eyes of the beholder? So maybe this is the same." She patted Susan's hands. "One thing I know for sure. Matt's goodness is inside her. And that's enough for me."

And with that, Susan burst into tears.

This was not turning out to be a good day. Therefore, the evening couldn't be worse.

The dress fit perfectly. Shannon nodded at herself in the mirror, then selected the blue shawl she'd bought in Texas to use inside the ballroom. With the cold outside temperature, however, she had to depend on her everyday parka for warmth.

"Maddy do it?" asked Maddie, who'd been watching the entire make-up and dress-up routines. Nearly forgotten routines.

"Mommy will do it for you," she said, pretending to brush some blush on her cheeks. "And you look so pretty in your new pajamas."

"Mommy and Maddie bof pretty."

Maddie's serious contemplation of her "big girl" pajamas set her laughing. "C'mon, let's show grandma and grandpa what a cute granddaughter they have in your new pj's."

The couple was chatting in the living room, but when she and Madison walked in, they fell silent. Susan's mouth slowly gaped open. John rose to his feet.

"You look just lovely, Shannon."

"Pj's, Grandpa."

"Wow! Look at you, Maddie!" John said, scooping up his granddaughter and tickling her belly.

Susan rose, her gazed moving over Shannon from head to foot. "You do look beautiful, Shannon. The dress is great. So are the earrings. And the hair-do and make-up." Her breath quavered, and Shannon could see in her eyes what was going through her mind.

She took a deep breath and glanced at her watch. Susan wasn't thinking straight—she was sure of it—and although Shannon's heart ached for the couple, if she were ever to go forward with her own life, she had to take a stand.

"I think I know what's on your mind, Susan. I can almost see the wheels turning in your head." She lowered her voice, gathered her courage and forced herself to look her mother-in-law in the eye. "You have to know that I totally loved your son. He'll never be forgotten as long as I live. But I'm thirty-one years old, Susan. And Maddie and I can't be hermits forever. It's not healthy. My brother will be here in two minutes to pick me up. But if you want, we can talk more about how I think you're feeling tomorrow."

She turned to face her father-in-law, who'd said nothing. "You can help me out here, John…." she began. But his brow wrinkled, and he looked worried before bestowing more kisses on Maddie.

Inhaling deeply again, Shannon said, "Let's turn this situation around for a moment. How would you feel if I were your daughter? A young widow. What would you advise her about all the years she had remaining?"

She hated to do it, hated to cause that stricken look on Susan's face.

A car horn sounded outside. "Okay, then. Dan's here and I'm off." She glanced at Susan, then Maddie. "Sweetheart, can you sing grandma a song? I bet she'd love to hear you sing."

As Shannon grabbed her Nikon and walked to the door, she turned back to see Maddie performing and Susan smiling. *Baby Beluga* was a winner.

##

"I'm so glad to see you both," said Shannon, after she'd seated herself in the back of Daniel's SUV. How are you, Sara?"

"Happy you're getting out tonight," replied her sister-in-law.

"It's a minor miracle," said Shannon. "Getting away was tough. Matt's mother…when she saw me dressed up…" She shook her head. "Let's just say, I'm glad for the two-hour distance between our homes."

Sara turned around to look at her. "I can imagine. Maybe you should have let Maddie stay with our kids tonight. Our sitter is great, and her folks live across the street. Nice backup if she ever needs help."

"Maybe next time," said Shannon, reaching to squeeze Sara's hand. "Thank you."

"No thanks needed," said Dan. "I'm proud of you, sis. Really. Too bad your in-laws didn't have more children. Regardless, I know for sure that Matt is cheering you on. That's what a man would do when—when he loves someone as Matt loved you." His last words were soft and sincere.

"Now I need tissues," Shannon choked out. "And my make-up is smearing. But…you really think so? Matt's rooting for me?"

"Of course, he is!" said Dan. "Your husband was not a selfish man. I'd like to think he and I were friends, and I know he'd want the best for you—in all ways—if you get my drift."

Oh, she got his drift. Dan's inference hit her like a speeding train, conjuring up an image of Andy Delaney in her mind. In the time she'd been trying to start over, she'd never once asked herself if Matt would approve of her decisions. She simply or not-so-simply made them. Until now, however, she'd never been faced with the question of a possible new relationship.

They were approaching the hotel now, and Dan pulled into the parking garage and found a spot.

"Ready, ladies?" he asked, offering an arm to each of them.

"This is going to be fun!" said Sara.

"Promise?" asked Shannon. "I feel like I have two left feet and a very bad case of butterflies, but onward we go."

CHAPTER SIX

She heard the music while walking toward the ballroom. Happy, upbeat and it made her want to dance. Humming along, she began to relax. It seemed the Delaney family wanted everyone in a good mood from the moment they arrived.

Table assignment cards rested on several podiums near the door. Before Shannon's party had a chance to search, however, she heard her dad's voice and Andy's voice calling her name simultaneously.

"Geez. They've got me in stereo," she said, waving to her father and turning to find Andy striding the hall toward them, a welcoming smile on his face that was hard to miss. He, himself, was hard to miss, filling out his tuxedo to dazzling perfection.

"Wow," she said as he approached. "You clean up really well. And a boutonniere in your lapel, too."

His warm laughter surrounded the little group as he enlightened her. "It's my auction notice. You'll see other single guys wearing them, too." He turned to her brother and extended his hand. "How are you, Dan? It's been a long time since I've been in, but I'm guessing business is good."

"Because we supply quality products that last," Dan replied with a wide smile. "We also, I might add, do the best work in the city." He introduced Sara, then asked, "What's this about an auction?"

"You'll find out all about it inside."

Her folks approached, her mom with arms outstretched. "Look at you, my love. So beautiful." Tears welled in her eyes. "I've been waiting for this."

Shannon produced a tissue from her purse. "Take it easy, Mom."

"But she's absolutely right," said Andy, reaching for Shannon's hand. "You look more than beautiful. Stunning."

He wanted to kiss her. She sensed it, but was happy he restrained himself. "Andy and I bumped into each other last week," she explained to the others, eyeing each of them. "You may not remember, but he and I worked on the high school newspaper together. Very intense experience, but rewarding, too."

"Wonderful," said Helen. "Can't have too many friends."

"On that note," said Andy, "I'd like to steal Shannon away and reintroduce her to some old friends. We'll make the rounds."

Dan's brows rose. "That sounds great. She's starting a new life in Boston. Hopefully, a happy one."

"That's my goal, too."

Her brother's eyes locked with hers in question. She gently shrugged, remembering once more how sharp Dan was. Another guy who noticed details.

Andy led them all back to the Murphy table, near the front of the room and close to the dance floor—right behind the reserved tables for his family.

"Very convenient," she joked, "for keeping your eye on your special bidder."

"Are you kidding? I'm not taking any chances."

She lifted the bidding paddle from the table, the number 5 marked in large print. "Isn't that the number on your uniform?"

"Yup." His gaze traveled toward the stage, where his siblings were starting to gather. "And then there were five," he said softly.

Five kids. She put her arm around him. "I get it."

After leaving her purse, shawl and camera on her chair, Shannon joined him in "making the rounds."

Andy was good to his word. "Look who I ran into on Newbury Street," he began each introduction. "Shannon is living back in town now." He was like her personal tour guide, but instead of pointing out a collection of art, he pointed out people.

She found herself chatting with two women she'd once known when they were all teens and forgot about her own situation as she caught up with Elise and Michelle and their husbands, jobs, children. Her nervousness dissipated in proportion to the rising noise level in the room as more guests arrived.

"My sister is signaling me," said Andy. "It's time for the debut of the Delaney Family Children's Foundation."

Shannon turned toward the others. "I'm so glad to reconnect. Please don't leave tonight until we can exchange phone numbers. Okay with you?"

"Absolutely," said a very pregnant Elise. "We'd love to meet your little one. I have a three-year-old daughter at home."

"We do playgroups," said Michelle. "My son's the same age, so it's a good match."

"Perfect," said Shannon, "although Maddie's in daycare while I go to work. But we'll figure it out. Friends are important, I think, for all ages."

She followed Andy back to her table. "Hang on a sec while I thank you. I'm glad I came and met up with those girls again, or rather women. Seems like yesterday...."

"Friends and family make a life," he said. "And now here comes my sister. Looks like I'm in trouble!"

A striking woman with long, wavy, auburn hair approached. Her eyes sparkled and her hand gestured in an impatient *come on* motion. "I expected nonchalance from Brian," she said, "not from you! Let's go."

He turned toward Shannon and held up his hands in defeat. "This one's Jen, and she's bossy like Lisa. The only nice sister is Emily, who you might remember. She was just a year behind you in school."

"Hi there," said Jen with a beautiful smile. "Thanks for coming. But I really have to take him away now. The room's almost full and we can't keep guests waiting."

"Go, go," said Shannon, waving Andy away with a laugh. "I know all about siblings."

Once seated, she kept her eyes on him and the activity in front of the room. When the band played *Take Me Out to the Ballgame,* she sat up straight.

"What? In the middle of a sophisticated affair?" she asked aloud. Then she laughed, realizing how appropriate the tune was for a sports-invested family. She picked up her camera with its new roll of twenty-four shots. Wasting even one was not an option. If she chose well, Andy's family could use the pictures for promotional purposes next year. An excellent way to say thank-you.

##

Andy sat with his brother, sisters, and their spouses, watching Mike Brennan take control of the evening. He was a natural choice for emcee, now that he worked in broadcasting and had been playing football in front of thousands of people all his adult life. Come to think of it, crowds didn't faze any of his sibs. Lisa in front of court, Emily on violin in front of live audiences, Jen…hmm…just naturally bossy and afraid of nothing, while he and Brian…poof! Working a stadium crowd came easily at this point.

He sat back, ready to appreciate the vision Mike and Lisa had put together for this audience. Ready to see and hear it articulated live instead of watching Lisa write and delete many times on her computer. He'd offered to help, but she'd turned him down. That's when he realized she was the same woman now as then, wanting to shoulder the bulk of responsibility. As far as he knew, she'd always succeeded.

He paid attention as Mike welcomed their guests, as he explained that the special event—the bachelor auction—would occur between dinner and dessert, and that when the band played *Take Me Out to the Ballgame,* it meant to pay attention to important announcements. "Wine and hors d'oeuvres are on your tables, so please enjoy as the love of my life, Lisa Delaney-Brennan, introduces you to the Robert and Grace Delaney Foundation for Children."

The love of his life. Well said, Michael, and certainly true.

Now Andy leaned forward, waiting for the polite applause to fade, and wondering what his big sister would say to these supporters. He hoped it was brief and not too personal. But you never knew with Lisa. She was a terrier at times, never letting go. And with her eye on

65

the prize tonight—winning over the crowd by explaining the Foundation's goals—he had no idea what to expect.

He caught Lisa's eye and gave her a thumbs-up. She grinned and he exhaled a long breath. He might only be her pain-in-the-ass brother, but he was on her team.

"Our sincere thanks to all of you for supporting this new venture and our very first fundraising event," Lisa began. "The entire Delaney family is very excited to be helping children whose parents are no longer with them. Whether being raised by a single parent, grandparents, guardians, or as in our case, sort of raising ourselves, these fragile families need support.

"We five Delaney kids lost our parents over twenty years ago. You may know some of us, but just in case…." One by one, she pointed at his siblings and introduced them. He stood when his turn came, waved to the crowd and sat again, glad he wasn't giving the speech. The room seemed as full as Fenway—where he didn't mind the spotlight.

"Our parents died," continued Lisa, "due to a car accident in the middle of January. There was almost no traffic, but it was dark, the road covered with black ice. Our lives…umm…changed in an instant. Changed forever."

Her voice shook and she paused again. Andy started to rise and join her, but Mike stepped forward and took her hand. A better choice. *The love of his life.*

When Lisa began speaking again, she sounded stronger. "It might seem to you that twenty years is long enough. Long enough to get over it. Long enough to push it aside. Long enough to forget. But I'm here to tell you that the reverberations of that fateful accident remain to this day. We don't forget. But we move forward with our lives. At least, we try to."

She paused again. Andy sat close enough to see her eyes well. *Oh, Lis. Don't go too deep.*

"The thing of it is," she said with a catch in her voice, "we were always trying to make them proud of us."

God almighty. She never listened to him anyway.

"Our purpose is to focus on the children. Here are some reasons why: twenty years ago, Jennifer was always running away and wanted to be emancipated, Emily threw up constantly, Brian swaggered with bravado, and Andrew shared nothing with us. At least not verbally. Your hometown Red Sox hero doesn't know it yet, but tonight is different. Tonight, we're opening a window into the mind of a real child so you can understand how a kid sees a broken world. And then I'll tell you about how the funds we raise are going to be used." She caught his eye. "Sorry, Andy. I'll explain later."

To his disbelief, Andy watched Lisa hold up an envelope. A very familiar- style envelope. He heard her read the address:

Robert and Grace Delaney
Heaven
The Universe

No, she couldn't! He hadn't thought about those letters in years, but still…they were private!

Dear Mom and Dad,

Can you hear us up in heaven? Can you see us? We have moved from Woodhaven to Boston, and that's a hundred miles. We don't know if you can find us now. Emily thinks yes, but she still believes in Santa Claus, so she's not credible. Did you notice my new vocabulary word? Mike says he never knows what's coming out of my mouth next.

There are six people in this house, but it feels empty without you. When we're really sad, Brian and I snuggle under Dad's wooly sweater. It still smells like him. And that feels good. I'm glad I'm a twin with Brian.

I still don't talk to the shrink, but I'll write again soon.

Love from your son,
Andy

Silence filled the ballroom. The huge ballroom. Andy's hands fisted, his breath choked. He sat frozen to his chair, tension rising, until he was ready to explode. Until he sensed Shannon's presence, inhaled the light fragrance she'd worn, felt her hand covering his own, comforting him. His fist loosened, and her fingers twined with his. Somehow, she'd pulled her chair from the adjacent table behind his and was now sitting close to him.

"How could she?" he murmured.

"Hang in there, Andrew," she whispered. "It's actually a beautiful testament to your parents and how they raised you with so much love."

"Just wait 'til later."

Shannon inched closer and whispered, "I'd want Maddie to feel just like you did. That she had a wonderful mom." She clasped her other hand around their interlocked ones, and Andy relaxed a bit more.

Hopefully Lisa was winding down. "When I found his first letter, it was sealed and stamped. And for the next year or so, the same. Eventually, however, the stamps were eliminated. I think Andy had figured out that letters to heaven were…free."

He heard Shannon chuckle, heard the other soft laughs nearby.

"So smart, even then," she whispered.

He'd merely been trying to survive, but if Shannon wanted to think he was smart, he wasn't going to argue the point, especially not there and then.

"I practice family law," Lisa said, "which includes parental death and guardianships, divorces and custody, termination of parental rights, adoptions as well as domestic violence cases. I've seen it all, and a lot of it is not pretty. I'm proud to say that some seed money for the Delaney Foundation has already gone to help several children for psychological services and after-school care.

"Each child is precious and unique, but in the end, these kids are also victims. They are powerless. We are reaching out, statewide, to give more of them a fighting chance for a good and secure life. They depend on caring adults to get them through. And that's where you come in."

Andy shifted to see Shannon better. "There's her pitch."

"It's a good one," she said. "That letter of yours helped make it personal. Children *are* victims, they *are* powerless, and they do need good adults in their corner."

She seemed as fierce as Lisa now. Perhaps that speech had hit too close to home. "Maddie has a fabulous mom," he said, "and look over there." He nodded toward the Murphy table. "She has lots of loving adults to spoil her."

He heard her sigh. "You're right, of course you're right. Thanks for reminding me."

Dancing began again, but as Andy rose, he said, "I still have a bone to pick with Lisa."

"Let it go, Andy. She's worked so hard to pull this off. Mike, too."

"I know that, and I'll be gentle," he replied. "I promise. Save the next dance for me."

"Sounds like a song."

"Right. You know what? Save all the dances for me."

##

He left her at her family's table and was striding to the front of the room when he felt a tap on his shoulder. Brian.

"Let's take it outside, bro."

"It's Lisa I want."

"Not yet. First, you and I."

Andy pivoted and stared into a pair of green eyes identical to those he'd see in his own mirror. Except now Brian's were shadowed with concern.

"I'm not going to cause a scene, if that's what you're worried about," Andy said, leading the way to the hall beyond the ballroom.

"That was one of my thoughts," said Brian, "but my more important concern was you. If one letter, one remembrance can affect you so much...then..."

"Then what? I'm not over the trauma? Fancy-schmancy words."

"None of us will ever be over the shock. But..."

"She should have asked me, Bri. At least warned me. I didn't need a blast from the past slamming me in the face with hundreds of people looking on. That's all."

Brian stayed quiet for a moment, and Andy could almost see his brain shuffling ideas as quickly as he could shuffle a deck of cards.

"About asking you first," Brian began. "I get it. But think about this for a moment..." His brow furrowed, his mouth tightened, and his hand went to Andy's shoulder and rested there.

"Twenty-three years ago," Brian said, "she asked the most important question of all, a question that, truthfully, made life harder on her. And she asked us first."

Andy waited while his brother paused his speech. Brian wasn't usually at a loss for words, but now he seemed to be picking them carefully.

"It was cold, and the house was crowded with visitors for days after the funeral," Brian said. "And one night, we all went outside to the front porch to get away. Remember? Just the five of us. And that was when she asked the crucial question. Do we want to stay together or live with our aunts and uncles? That was the heart of the matter."

"Of course, I remember," Andy replied. "We all said yes, stay together, and she had to fight for us in court. Mike was there, too, but they weren't married."

"In that situation, lots of siblings would be separated, Andy. But she let a couple of nine-year-olds, a seven-year-old and a teenager make the choice. So, if you can think of that ask as a silver lining, give Lis a break."

A kaleidoscope of memories and thoughts tumbled through Andy's mind until…. "And now we've established the Delaney Foundation for Children. And Lisa's still fighting for children, using every piece of ammunition she can find, including my little-boy letter."

Brian's slow smile was comforting. "But this time, she's got a grown-up Delaney army at her side. Right?"

Andy stared straight into his brother's eyes. "As I wrote to Mom and Dad twenty years ago, 'I'm glad I'm twins with Brian.'"

A big clap on the back. "It's mutual, bro. It's mutual."

"Hi boys…" called Lisa.

"Boys?" asked Andy, surprised he could joke. "Brian just said we're grown-ups!"

She waved the comment away. "Before I find the ladies' room, I want to apologize to you, Andy, for not asking your permission about that letter. I was truly drowning in all the preparations and forgot. But I'm glad you understand."

"How do you know that?"

"Oh, puleeze," she said with a dismissive motion. "You're both laughing, so life is good. What more proof do I need?" She waved and headed toward her destination.

"Man, oh, man, she knows us well," said Andy. "Sometimes, too well." He spotted Shannon at the doorway and motioned her over.

"She really thinks she's our mom," Brian offered. "Or a version of."

"Here's another mom who's figuring it all out. Do you remember…"

"Shannon Murphy!" Brian exclaimed. "Of course. Still taking pictures?"

She grinned and nodded. "You bet. In fact, I've got my camera with me tonight. Good to see you, Brian." She shook his hand.

"Shannon's moved back to town with her little daughter," said Andy, "and I talked her into coming tonight and having some fun."

"My family bought a table," she said.

"I see…" mused Brian, looking from one to the other. "So, are you bidding on this guy?" he asked, tilting his head toward Andy.

"You'd be surprised," said Andy.

"Brian, if your wife's the one with the honey-blonde hair, I think she wants to dance," said Shannon. "She's using a chair as a partner."

Brian immediately disappeared back into the ballroom as Shannon touched Andy's arm.

"Is everything okay with Lisa?"

"More than okay. You were right. She apologized for not asking my permission to read it. She'd meant to. I'm glad I didn't jump down her throat."

"I knew you'd figure it out. Now—are you ready to chance my stepping on your feet?" Shannon challenged with a wry laugh. "I haven't been on a dance floor in...a very long time."

"I'm not worried at all," Andy replied, leading her back inside. "But If I step on your toes in those sexy sandals...? Now that would be a problem."

LINDA BARRETT

CHAPTER SEVEN

She hadn't thought about Matt all evening until she was dancing in Andy's arms. And then it hit – she was being held closely by someone who was not her husband. Dancing with a man who was not her husband.

Similar yet different. With both men, she could count on a quick smile. Matt's greater height and trimmer physique contrasted with Andy's fit, more defined body and powerful shoulders. Light on his feet. Suddenly, her head throbbed, and her regular breaths became gasps. The evening was becoming as difficult as she'd imagined it would be. Her happy time hadn't lasted very long.

The song changed. Several female vocalists took the lead, creating beautiful harmony.

"Another family affair," said Andy, turning her gently toward the stage.

"Holy Toledo! All three of them?" she asked, distracted by the sight of Lisa, Jen and Emily wowing the audience with their version of *Stand by Me.*

"That's their theme song. Goes way back."

"I can imagine. It's very appropriate. And they've got the audience still dancing and sort of singing along."

"And that's a good thing," he said, holding her closer. "I like dancing with you. How are your feet so far? Have I crushed them yet?"

The man could make her laugh—*and that's also a good thing.* Her confidence returned. "I'm glad I came," she said, "and I'll confess you weren't the only one with a tough moment tonight. I had a couple myself just now, but you're making it easy for me again."

"My pleasure," he said, bestowing a quick kiss on her temple. "Anytime, anyplace, anything. I'm a good listener."

When the band played *Take Me Out to the Ballgame,* they headed back to their tables. Dinner was being served.

"Here we are, only a few feet apart," she said, as Andy pulled her chair out and chatted with her family for a minute.

"Hey, Shan?" he said, pointing at the table top. "Where's the bidding paddle? I don't see it, and you know that crazy event is coming next."

One glance moved to another all around the Murphy table. "Not to worry," said Helen, pushing her chair back and reaching down. "We wanted more surface room, so I put it on the floor." She placed it in front of Shannon's dinner plate, her eyes shifting from her daughter to Andy. "Glad to know it will be used!"

"Absolutely," said Shannon. "With so many attractive, eligible hotties available…."

She watched seven jaws drop at the table and knew she'd hit the mark. Laughter bubbled up and she grinned. "That'll stop you from jumping to conclusions."

"Such a joker! Now you're just teasing me," said Andy softly to her. "But I can handle it. Just make sure to ignore the other hotties and focus on this one!"

##

The local professional disc jockeys wasted no time in getting the auction off to a blazing start. A quick general patter set the mood.

"Take a good look, ladies! These guys are on fire…to raise lots of money for kids, so let's make sure they do."

To the strong beat of *It's Raining Men,* vocalized by the Delaney sisters, fifteen bachelors with their carnation boutonnieres paraded, danced, and walked across the stage.

"I wonder how many drinks they've had already…?" asked Sara, as she clapped in rhythm to the song.

"You couldn't get me to do that without a few belts," replied Dan. "But look at Andy Delaney, tossing that baseball in the air like he doesn't have a care in the world."

Catcalls and whistles came from all over the room.

Shannon grabbed her camera and started making the rounds—the singing Delaney sisters backed up by the band, shots of individual bachelors in whatever pose they struck, including Andy, who gave her a thumbs-up and a prize-winning grin. So much more extroverted than she. Her eye focused on anything that might show off the event and encourage more patrons to attend next year.

The babble from the DJ was over-the-top cute. "We're previewing the wares, ladies… your Prince Charming might be strutting in front of your eyes right now… step right up, and find your pick of the litter!"

To Shannon's disbelief, some of the women did go toward the stage for a closer look, perhaps solidifying their first impressions. All the potential bidders had mingled with the bachelors for a while earlier in the evening. Who knew? Maybe some would hit it off. She raised her camera and captured the scene.

The singing ended, and the band faded to a very low volume, just enough to prevent a total silence while the business of the auction started.

"Let's hear it for the fun-loving gentlemen on the stage this evening," said the DJ. "These guys have left their dignity at home for the sake of the kids who need help. We've got fifteen stand-up men to auction off. And the first one is…."

Shannon soon realized that Andy would be last. He wasn't the only popular sports pro in the group, so his last-place status was probably due to his co-hosting the event. As she listened to the bids being announced and watched the paddles being held up, she also realized that Andy would have no complaints about an approximate five- or six-hundred-dollar donation. He'd probably put up a lot more than that in seed money already. Her concerns about a sky-high bid evaporated.

The other bachelors were soon all spoken for, and before she knew it, Andy was up. The minute the bidding began, she realized she had competition. She couldn't see the other woman who was farther back, but knew she was in it when the DJ called her bid and table number.

In less than a minute, five hundred had been long passed. Nine hundred now. Shannon raised her paddle.

"Nine hundred to the little lady with Murphy Auto Parts."

"One thousand," called the other woman.

Perspiration dotted Shannon's skin. She didn't mind bidding, but hadn't counted on being under a spotlight. Like a tennis match. When the light followed the women, the guests looked from one to the other and back again. She glanced at Andy, who offered a slight nod.

In thirty seconds, the DJ got it up to fifteen hundred, and Shannon's paddle went up.

"Two thousand," called out the other woman, not waiting for the simple hundred-dollar increments.

There was only one thing for Shannon to do now. Cut her off at the pass. She didn't seek Andy's approval. No nod, no smile. Her paddle went up in the air. "Five thousand dollars," she sang out, her voice crisp and clear.

The buzz around the room! Her own parents looked at her in shock. "What are you doing? Five thousand?"

She ignored them all. Andy must have known something like this might happen. A passionate fan or a person who wanted something—maybe a favor of some kind—from him. She had no idea how famous ball players protected their privacy. She had an uneasy feeling, however, that there might be more to this particular bidding contest than a simple date.

She'd see it through despite the attention she was getting. Andy was worth protecting from whatever her competitor wanted.

The DJ looked toward the back of the room. "That's five thousand for the children." He paused, whether to increase the drama or give the woman a chance to think, Shannon didn't know. "Going once..."

"Six thousand," called the woman.

Only a twenty percent increase over the base. She's slowing down.

Shannon raised her paddle. "A cool ten thousand."

A mix of gasps and chuckles came from the audience, some applause, too.

"Oh, those children have a mama," crooned the DJ, again looking toward the back. "That's ten thousand dollars, going once…"

Silence.

"Going twice…. Are we done?" And the gavel came down. "A date is made between power hitter Andy Delaney and Ms. Power Bidder Murphy Auto Parts!"

Good enough. But she couldn't move. Could hardly breathe. Her family looked confused. Worried. Amazed. Only her gramps was laughing.

"What a night! Shannon, my girl. I didn't know you had it in ya'."

I don't.

"For that money," Frank continued, "tell him to up our Fenway tickets to full season!"

She sensed Andy's presence before hearing his voice. "Done! A full season for you, Mr. Murphy. Shannon saved me from wasting an evening."

"Do you know the other lady?" asked Sara.

"Not a clue. Reminded me of a persistent reporter after a story or someone with something on her mind. I've been around plenty of both in my life." He leaned over, reached for Shannon's hands, and she rose. "You were wonderful, Shan. I'm forever in your debt."

"Debt is the word," said Helen. "I think she's in your debt to the tune of ten thousand dollars. Wow."

Andy stared intently at her mother. "The only debt Shannon has is to go out to dinner with me. I'm covering the bid."

Her mother's expression changed from woe to interest as she looked from Andy to her and back again.

"Just like a photograph being processed, I think this picture is getting a bit clearer." She waved toward the dance floor. "Go have fun."

"Yes, ma'am," said Andy, leading Shannon to the dance floor and taking her in his arms.

##

Not a bad place to be, she thought, as Andy held her closely. The band had slowed the tempo, and she recognized the Bee Gees' *Massachusetts* wafting in the air around them. Nice choice for this crowd of Bay Staters.

Her calm ended with the end of the song.

"Uh-oh," said Andy. "I think we're in for a bit of trouble. Here's your competitor coming toward us."

The woman seemed a cross between angry and upset, and was definitely on a mission. Not as glamorous up close as some of the other ladies, and certainly not as carefree.

"You two seem very comfortable with each other," she said. "Was it a fair bidding?"

Behind his blazing eyes, Shannon sensed Andy's shocked restraint as he took in the woman's appearance.

"It's for charity," he said calmly. "The children are benefitting by an extra four thousand dollars."

"But my son isn't!" she cried. "That's all I wanted. Some reserved time so you would visit my son. You're his favorite Red Sox player. When you fly around the bases, he's with you in spirit, but he can barely walk from his bed to the bathroom when his arthritis flares. Only eight years old and-and he has to cope."

In her passion, she'd started to tear up. "Oh! What's the point?" She waved sharply toward the band and the crowd. "Have a great time." She turned to go.

"Hang on a minute," said Andy. "Not so fast."

The woman paused, then followed as he led them all off the dance floor.

"Let's start with this," Andy said. From his pocket, he took out the baseball he'd been tossing earlier. From inside his jacket, he pulled out a pen.

"What's your son's name?"

From despair to joy. "Chris. Chris Barnes. I'm Terri Barnes, by the way."

He glanced at Shannon. "Can you get Brian and Mike over here?"

Andy was in business mode, problem-solving mode, and Shannon had full confidence this incident would be resolved well.

Five minutes later, young Chris Barnes had a rare baseball signed by the top starting pitcher for the Houston Astros as well as by his favorite hometown player.

"And now Mike Brennan will sign it as well." He turned toward the man he loved like a dad, and said, "Put 'signatures verified by Mike Brennan, QB."

Then he looked at Terri. "This is one-of-a-kind. Give it to Chris, but then put it in a safe place. It's your financial backup just in case you need it."

If her eyes got any wider, they'd pop out. "I'd never, ever sell this. It will make Chris so happy." The tears finally fell.

Shannon felt like crying, too. "You're another lioness taking care of her cub. Just like me. I'd never sell it either."

"Thank you so much," Terri said with a quizzical glance at Shannon. "I never expected...never...he's at Boston Children's now. I'll see him tomorrow."

Andy glanced at Brian, who nodded. "And so will we," Andy told the woman, to her astonishment.

Brian added, "I'll tell Meggie to notify the Stros' organization. They like to keep track."

"Megan's right here," said Brian's wife. "You can tell her yourself."

Shannon enjoyed the give-and-take between Andy's brother and his wife. Lovely couple. And now young Chris Barnes would be getting visitors the next day. Such an unselfish act for both brothers. Shannon listened to Andy chat with Terri a little longer, heard the woman mention that her friends who came that night had all backed Terri's bid at the auction. It made sense to Shannon that a single mom would need that kind of help. She tracked them both as Andy escorted Terri back to her table.

"Your eyes are glowing," Megan said. "Andy's a wonderful guy, but seems to prefer the single life, living in Florida part-time, never bringing a woman home for us to meet. Maybe things are changing now…?"

"It's not even been two weeks," said Shannon.

"Time's a funny thing. In any case, I hope we see each other again," Megan said warmly before hurrying off.

I hope so, too.

No doubt running into Andy Delaney had opened her life up in many ways, including her attendance at this gala. No more hiding away, dismissing all men because they weren't her late husband. If tonight was a test of maintaining blind loyalty to Matt, she'd failed. She'd actually enjoyed herself, and hoped Matt was up there somewhere rooting for her, as her brother had suggested.

She thought of Andy's letter to his folks that Lisa had read aloud. Maybe now, she would be the one writing a letter to heaven—if only in her mind.

If the evening she'd initially dreaded had proved anything at all, it was that her life was beginning again. It might include Andy—a happy thought—or it might not. But she'd now stepped out of her comfort zone and into the fray.

CHAPTER EIGHT

"Shannon seems like a winner to me—and to Megan."

From behind the wheel, Andy glanced at his twin, reclining in the passenger seat, eyes closed, after they pulled away from Boston Children's. The visit to young Chris Barnes had been a home run. They wound up staying longer to provide some fun for other kids on the floor as well. A good pick-me-up for parents and offspring on a drab Sunday afternoon in a place they'd rather not be.

"Megan, too? Then you must be right."

"I am. Just don't know if she's the winner for you. Or you for her, for that matter."

Andy looked over again, saw an eyelid half-raised, and knew Brian was poking for a reaction to his comment.

"I've got a ticket to Miami for this Wednesday."

"You're a fool if you use it. And now I'm done."

A man of few words, his brother. Not an orator, not a writer. Just a happy man with a beautiful family who'd literally fought for his Megan. And in doing so, revived his flailing pitching career with a couple of no-hitters—a rare feat.

"Every guy who falls in love thinks everyone else should do the same." Andy smiled wryly. "I've seen it over and over with my friends, and you're no different."

"But I am different," said Brian. "You got another twin walking around somewhere? No, you don't," he answered himself. "And I know where you're coming from. Been there myself."

"So now we have revelations from the heart? I'll ask Emily to play her violin."

"Sarcasm. Another defense. I know them all. And I know what I saw last night. You couldn't take your eyes off Shannon Murphy—always looking, always checking. Hell, bro, you smiled the whole time, except for the letter business."

"Shannon Roberts." Had he?

"Dang it, Andy. You looked happy, damned happy. And I'm pretty sure it wasn't an act."

"I thought you were done talking."

"As long as you're not done thinking."

She was only on his mind twenty-four seven. But Brian didn't need to know everything.

Thirty minutes later, they entered the house on Beacon Street where they'd been raised by Lisa and Mike. A small tornado greeted them at the door.

"Dad-dy, Dad-dy. I'm here!" Little Gracie Robin launched herself at Brian, who swept her up as easily as a slow grounder.

"There's my girl." A dozen kisses were bestowed while he kept her in his arms. His eyes searched the room.

"Megan's there," said Andy, pointing to the sofa, where his sister-in-law napped.

"Mom's exhausted," said a young voice, and I'm taking care of Gracie."

"Good," said Brian, reaching for his adopted son. "Can't think of a better substitute...except for me. Or maybe not!"

Andy took in the whole scene. So much love and devotion...but so much risk. Brian's whole heart had been given. But what if tragedy struck again?

How easily he'd urged Shannon to rejoin society. Socialize. Meet old friends. Make new friends. Glib words. Cheap talk.

"Mom's still in her pajamas." His niece, Briana, stepped toward Andy. "How was the party last night? Mom and Dad were too tired to talk."

"Went very well, sweetheart," he replied, hugging her close. "We raised a lot of money, everyone danced, your mom and aunties sang with the band and were a big hit."

And I held a wonderful woman in my arms.

"Did you take pictures?" Briana asked. "I want to see them singing. And Mom and Dad dancing. Next year, I should go. I'll be twelve by then."

"Not my call, baby. Thank goodness."

"You'd say yes," she replied. "You always say yes to everything we want to do." She leaned into his chest and wrapped her arms around him. "I love you, Uncle Andy. I'm so glad you're home now."

He melted. "I love you, too, Briana. Right in here." He tapped the left side of his chest. "And that goes for your brother and..." He looked at Brian's kids, Josh and Gracie, thought about Jen's twins, Lily and Laura, thought about the excitement—and stress—of their births, thought about growing up in this house, the great emotional struggles tempered by great loyalty right from the start. His siblings had been everything to each other. Together, they'd stumbled through the worst and made the best of it. But not without scars. Brian's trade to the Houston Astros had hit Andy in the gut. The adult Andy.

Nothing lasts forever. So why look for more trouble? He'd been in a good place for a while now.

His gaze rested on one beloved face after another. Should another face be there? One with cornflower blue eyes. He sighed deeply. The joke was on him. Love involved more risk than pro sports. Didn't it? Bad things happened that you couldn't control. No guarantees. No safety net. Just risk…and perhaps another topic for his readers to ponder.

But maybe he'd postpone his trip and hope he wouldn't be sorry.

##

She hadn't heard from Andy at all on Sunday, and perhaps that was just as well. Maddie had climbed out of her crib and crawled onto the sofa at zero-dark-thirty and Shannon's day began with four hours sleep. By eight o'clock that evening, she was in her own pj's, toying with the idea of developing the pictures she'd taken last night, or going to bed with a book.

Her cell rang. No decision needed. She checked the readout and smiled.

"Big day for you, too?" she asked.

"More than you can imagine," Andy replied. "First the hospital visit, and now I'm helping Jen handle finances for the Foundation. A lot of rules and regs, but it's worth it."

"You just helped me make up my mind. I'll be heading to the basement after we hang up. Never too soon to plan for next year's promotion."

"I like the sound of that. I had a great time last night, Shannon, even with the extra drama."

"I did, too, Andy. I'm glad you talked me into 'saving you.' If I'm there next year, however, I'll need different baby-sitters. Susan's cross-examination when I got home belonged in a court of law. It was funny and sad at the same time. A little soap opera, but mixed with pain and confusion. I really don't know what to do about my mother-in-law or how to help her." And she didn't want Susan's needs to dictate her own choices. Ugh. Life could be complicated.

"Is it your responsibility? It sounds like she needs to help herself at this point. We all went to therapy early on. Doesn't the military have provisions for Gold Star families?"

"It certainly does. I started to mention it, but she cut me off." In her mind's eye, she pictured how all the wives had gathered round her when she found out about Matt. In fact, the entire support system had shown up.

"When Matt died, I was never alone," she mused. "But I was living on base, and his parents aren't. Maybe I can put a bug in John's ear to reach out to local veterans' groups. Thanks for reminding me, Andy. My shoulders feel a little lighter."

"I'm glad to help in any way I can. I hope you know that."

"I-I do, but sometimes I'm not sure why. You don't know me very well yet."

"Don't I? Regardless of all you've gone through, you haven't changed much from the girl I remember. But I'm very willing to put your concerns to rest. Go out with me—you and Maddie—starting tomorrow after work. I'll pick you both up at the house, and we'll get some dinner."

She liked the way he automatically included Maddie. "As long as daycare tells me she's napped. Otherwise, a restaurant dinner will be a disaster."

"In that case, we'll bring it inside. I'll pick up something. Sound like a plan?"

Was she getting too comfortable with him? Would Maddie start getting too comfortable? "Call me tomorrow afternoon, and I'll let you know where we stand."

"I'm taking that as a yes."

She disconnected after saying goodnight, wondering at the signals Andy was sending. Clear signals. Well, forewarned was forearmed.

The next evening, Chinese food take-out containers and paper plates filled the table in Shannon's kitchen.

"If we keep doing this, I'll gain weight in front of both our eyes," said Shannon, holding her tummy after the meal.

"Mmmm," hummed Maddie contentedly, enjoying the bits of Chinese delicacies her mother has arranged on her high chair tray.

He looked at Maddie. "I think you and your Mommy both like this meal. Is it good?"

Maddie grinned wide enough to show off her teeth. Then came the yawns. And tears.

"I think an early bedtime," said Shannon.

"No. No. Not tired. No bed yet!"

Andy looked and sounded totally bewildered. "Laughing one minute, crying the next."

"Which means she's overtired but doesn't know it. This isn't going to be pretty, my friend."

"An—dee, An—dee. No sleep yet." The toddler looked up at him with adorable appeal, and Shannon watched him melt. He squatted in front of Maddie and carefully lifted her into his arms. He stood, crooned to her and waltzed her around the room.

"I think this is called playing one adult off against the other," said Shannon. "Not going to happen." Stroking Maddie's cheek, she took her from Andy's arms. "Andy will come say goodnight when you're ready."

"While you take on Maddie, I'll take on the kitchen cleanup."

"Thanks."

"Of course. And no thanks needed."

Ten minutes later, Shannon waved him inside the bedroom. Maddie was lying down, eyes half closed, but small shuddering sobs checked her breathing. Andy leaned over the crib and gently stroked her cheek.

Her lids came all the way down, her breathing became even and she slept.

As she watched the other two, Shannon's stomach tightened. Maddie was beginning to have an attachment to Andy. She was growing comfortable with him. Her earlier concern had merit. She'd heard and read stories about children of single moms latching on to every nice guy their moms dated. Not good for the kids to ride between hope and disappointment. She comforted herself that she'd been caught by surprise. A new relationship hadn't been on her radar at all. Now she realized it carried a very big risk, one she couldn't take for the sake of her daughter. She hoped Andy would understand.

##

He didn't. Abruptly standing after she spoke, his chair fell backwards to the kitchen floor. He didn't bother to right it.

"What kind of game is this, Shannon? With your working hours, daycare pickups, and a little one with early bedtimes—when would we see each other if Maddie's not included?"

"I understand what you're saying, but I promise, it's not a game." She stood as well, but didn't look or sound happy. "She really enjoys your visits, Andy. She likes you. And—and if we keep seeing each other, I'm afraid her feelings will grow."

"And that's a problem? I like her too. You're not making sense."

"It's all so new—this—this relationship we're in. We don't know where it's heading, and it's my job to play defense. I'm her mother. I don't want her confused or hurt."

He wasn't expecting drama, but he wasn't running from it either. "I thought you and Maddie were a package deal. That's what you said, and I'm still here. So why the change?" He paused as another possibility struck him. One he didn't want to consider and didn't believe. But he couldn't run now either.

"Look at me, Shannon, and give me a straight answer. I hope I'll hear the answer I want." He inhaled deeply. "Are you hiding behind Maddie in order to cool things off between us?" He couldn't believe that he'd been so bad at reading the signs.

She remained quiet, and his heart almost stopped beating until she slowly moved her head back and forth. "No. Definitely not that. Besides, I don't hide behind my daughter or anyone. I'm here, Andy. Toe-to-toe with you. But I'm not sure Maddie should come for the ride at this point."

Relieved but puzzled. A smart lady who made no sense. "You're changing the rules in the middle of the game, and I think, Shan, you're only fooling yourself. Odds are she'll ask about me whether you like it or not."

"Maybe for a while," Shannon replied, "but kids can forget if-if...mmm... you know what I mean. I'm sorry, Andy. This is a whole new chapter for me. And I have to get it right!"

Mike and Lisa hadn't done everything right, but he'd wound up okay. So had his siblings. "So where does that leave us?" he asked. "One Saturday night date a week? That's not enough. These few months are the off-season for me. At the end of February, my life won't be my own anymore."

Her mouth opened and closed. Her hand moved to the base of her throat.

"What? Why?"

Total confusion bathed her face. It was time to educate her about his career, and the reality behind the scenes. He finally righted his chair and waved at her to sit back in hers. "Let's get comfortable while I clue you in." He waited until she complied.

"In brief, the team starts with six weeks preseason training in Ft. Myers, Florida—a beautiful facility, by the way—then Opening Day, and the season starts for real. Of course, I'll be based in Boston with the team and live at home, but half the time we travel. There's a published schedule that everyone can follow. Players and fans. That's how it works."

Those big blue eyes widened in surprise. "I had no idea about any kind of training. I guess I've never thought about it." She leaned back in her chair and glanced at the ceiling. Her eyes closed, and furrows formed on her brow. "So...what you're saying is that you're away from home half the year." The furrows deepened. "Always away. Just like Matt."

A missile out of the blue. "It's not the same at all," Andy protested. "To start with, my life isn't at risk in a war. A worry that added to your burden. And moreover, many players' families come for the spring training time in Ft. Myers. They have second homes there or rent condos. Later, some pick and choose away games they want to attend. Different reasons—to visit cousins, go shopping, and see the game. So it's not the same at all."

She remained quiet.

He leaned across the table and took her hands. "I suppose it's a lot to process for someone with no knowledge of pro sports. And there's more, so you need time to think.

"I usually live in Miami during the off-season. Friends, weather, extra writing time, the whole bit. But this year was…different. I wasn't planning to go. And I've never cancelled those plans before."

She pursed her lips and regarded him soberly. "Because of me?" she whispered.

He stood and leaned against the fridge. Too much energy to contain. "Yeah. Why else? And just like you, I wanted to see where this thing between us was heading. How can that happen if we're twelve hundred miles apart? So I'd changed my mind about Miami." He paused, his thoughts racing. "But maybe I'll fly down there after all. The last thing I want to do is push you where you don't want to go."

"I'm sorry, but—"

He cut her off. "If we were strangers, meeting for the first time, I could understand your caution about Maddie. Maybe single parents should insist on at least six dates or something before meeting children. But we know each other a long time, so that horse has already left the barn."

He took a deep breath. Giving up was not his style. "Brian's wife, Megan, can tell you anything you want to know about baseball families…and kids. Brian adopted Josh. Their happiness spilled over on everyone, and we all celebrated with them.

"As far as handling life during the playing season," he said more quietly, "I guess you're the only one who can figure it out. Where does your happiness lie?"

He walked over to her and reached for her hand. She rose. "While I'm gone, and you're thinking about your new rules and regs, and about new relationships—our relationship—here's a head start." He drew her close and leaned down.

She didn't resist. In fact, she came closer, her hands around his neck, her head tilted back, making it easy for him to kiss her and leave his mark. *Don't forget me.* He covered her mouth hungrily, needing the taste, the sweetness. Wanting her to know his heart and for her to feel the same.

She sensed his desire, a craving that it seemed only she could satisfy. He was giving himself to her now, and she let her senses take over. She kissed him freely, this man who wanted her, but who'd wait for her. She savored every moment, the warmth, the eagerness, the shivers as well as the burn. This was good and right.

She breathed his name.

"I'm here."

She held him tight and then let go.

"Hopefully, Shan, this will be a short trip."

"No promises, but yes. Hopefully it will."

##

While waiting for his flight to board on Wednesday, Andy reached into his carry-on for the copy of Sunday's paper he'd saved to read at leisure. Especially the write-ups about the gala, which he'd only glimpsed at earlier in the week. He thumbed through until he got to the *Around the Town* section. And there was the spread about the fundraiser. Pictures of Mike, the hometown hero QB, chatting up the crowd. Shots of the entire

Delaney clan, and then a shot of the bachelors walking across the stage, including one Andrew Delaney right in the center.

He'd give the photographer credit for capturing the highlights, but he was sure Shannon's pictures would have been more effective. Not that he'd seen them, but she had the knack.

Scanning the articles beneath the photos, he nodded in approval about the write-ups. Clear descriptions of the foundation's goals. Good press.

Until he read about his particular auction, which of course, highlighted the excitement of the two women bidding on him.

Just what he didn't need. What Shannon didn't need. He could imagine their families pouncing on the story. But it seemed that privacy had no place when raising money.

He texted her a heads-up about the society column. She hadn't said anything about it, so maybe she didn't subscribe to the paper. But he'd be surprised if no one in her circle mentioned it to her.

Next, he caught up with the news and sports. Basketball, football, hockey. All in full season. He had several new ideas for *Beyond the Locker Room,* ideas that focused on the human side of sports. Seemed lots of people were as interested as he in life off the field. So many that over the years, the Globe had approached him for permission to reprint some of his essays.

In a few months, baseball would fill the sports pages. He wondered what his personal life would look like then.

CHAPTER NINE

Thanks for your text about the gala. My in-laws called
this afternoon while I was at the gallery. It wasn't pretty.
I took some deep breaths afterward.

Andy sat on the terrace of his condo in the early
evening, reading Shannon's message. From what she'd
told him about the couple, their reaction was to be
expected, and her reaction was understandable.

He stretched out on the cushioned chaise, enjoying
the breeze and the slight ocean fragrance that wafted
through the air. Soon he'd make some calls and catch up
with the guys. Maybe a poker game for the next night. In
the morning, he'd hit the gym. Get back to his daily
work-out routine and visits to the batting cages. Ten
years of enjoying a second home. His private retreat
away from the hecticness of his Boston life. A perfect
balance.

But he'd been ready to sell the condo and stay up north full-time—before his last conversation with Shannon.

It would still happen, if her response to him, his touch and kiss were anything to judge by. He sighed. If it were only that easy. Comparing his life to her husband's commitment—that was the bigger deal. And it just didn't make sense.

"Dammit," he breathed, jumping to his feet. He pulled on some running shoes and headed to the beach. Sitting around talking to himself wasn't going to change anything. Running a few miles was more his style, and would certainly clear his mind.

He left his phone in the apartment and established a steady pace on the hard sand near the shoreline. Problems began to fade after only a mile. By two miles he was flying free, and by three, he didn't feel the ground. Was totally into the zone. Five miles took him back to his door and into a hot shower.

He checked the time, then checked his intentions. Too early for Maddie to be down for the night. Other calls waited for his attention, however, and when they were done, he was set for that poker game the next evening, including dinner beforehand. His buddies were always happy to hear from him, and the single ones were always ready for some evening action, besides cards. He'd grinned at their enthusiasm and had given a muted response.

The one thought that saturated his brain was Shannon.

Time to connect.

She picked up immediately. "Hi. Glad you called."

"Miss me yet?"

Her genuine laugh made him smile. "Of course. How could I disappoint you by saying anything else?"

"Just stick to the truth, Shan. That's all."

"In that case, I have some great news. You're going to love the prints of the gala I've developed. I'm in my darkroom right now, and the one of your three sisters singing together is—I have to say it myself—outstanding."

"Do you have a good one of Mike? What Mike Brennan does gets noticed."

"I do. But don't undersell the rest of your clan. It's really amazing after such a tough start." Her voice trailed off, and he knew darker thoughts followed. He called her back to reality.

"How'd it go with your in-laws after that piece in the paper?"

"Before or after Susan accused me of being a horrible wife and a loose woman? And how could I make a scene like that in front of the whole world? Was I so desperate for another man that I offered to pay?"

"Geezuz, Shan. That was quite a mouthful." Maybe she was dealing with other stressors that were complicating her agenda.

"Yup. And I'm getting tired of it. If they won't call the veteran's service for a therapist, I will. Maybe someone can pay a visit."

"Great idea."

"Something's got to change. I promised to spend Christmas day and night with them."

"Oh, boy. You're being more than fair," he said. "You're a strong woman, Shan. I know you'll handle them, but it's too bad you need to. Sorry I can't help. But I know my presence would only set her off."

Silence. "For sure. But I've been thinking about our last conversation, Andy. You made some good points."

"Glad to hear that."

"But I did, too."

"And…?"

"And I don't know whether to listen to my heart or my head."

"Now we're getting somewhere! In the meantime, no pressure. I'll tell Mike to pick up the prints at the gallery. The whole family is very excited and very...touched by your generosity in offering the photos for publicity for the foundation."

"They must trust your judgement about my talent! And Mike's, too. The others haven't seen my work yet, but Lisa called to thank me anyway. I told her I was very happy to help in any way I can."

"That's so like you, Shan. Nothing like a great photo to draw attention. Thank you very much."

"For children in need...no thanks necessary."

He cleared his throat. "So, shall I tell Mike to pick up the prints at the gallery? Does that work for you?"

"Sure. I'll bring them with me tomorrow. And thank you, too."

"For what?"

"For your understanding and patience."

"Take all the time you need." He said the words but didn't mean them. Out of sight, out of mind? No way! He'd pull a few surprises so that old saying wouldn't work.

Two days later, it was Jennifer who showed up at the Greenburg Gallery. Shannon recognized her immediately—Andy's older sister with the striking auburn hair. The one in finance.

"So nice to see you again, Jennifer. I've got the photos in the back room. Come walk with me."

The woman lagged behind, however, staring from one display of art to another. "You've got some beautiful work here to tempt browsers."

Shannon paused her step. "We surely do. I love being part of it."

"I'm almost totally unfamiliar with the art world. What exactly do you do here?"

Shannon laughed. "Once I get started, you might be sorry you asked the question! I love it all—not only meeting and greeting visitors, but doing research on the artists, helping organize special events, and working on the computer systems. It's never boring. I'm lucky they took me on parttime. Usually no weekends."

"Doug and I have been in our home for about three years. Maybe it's time to think about this kind of stuff— now that the kids are grown up! A whopping five years old!"

The woman's grin brightened her whole face.

"I bet they make their own art," said Shannon, thinking of the happy mess Maddie made with her fingerpaints.

Jen's nose wrinkled. "If you can call it art…"

They entered the back office and Shannon carefully removed each photo from its own file, each one protected by special paper. "I knew the *Boston Globe* sent a photographer to cover the event, so that wasn't my goal," said Shannon. "I was always thinking about promoting next year's dinner-dance. See what you think."

She took out one at a time. First, the decorated room and table set-up. Small groups of guests, mingling. Then the family—Mike and Lisa; Andy and Brian; the five Delaney siblings; the five with Mike; four with spouses, with Andy centered; and then…the three sisters singing with the band.

Jennifer looked from one to the other, her small gasps of astonishment soon turning into tears. "Is-is that who we really are now? Have we finally reached our happily-ever-after?"

Shannon pushed a box of tissues across the table. "What do you mean?" she whispered.

"The Delaney children have come a very long way." Jennifer blinked quickly and patted her eyes. "Nothing's been easy, but"—she waved at the pictures— "you and your camera have shown us how beautifully a rocky road can end."

"Stop, please. You're making me cry, too!" Shannon grabbed a tissue and blew her nose.

Jen pulled out her cell phone and waited for the connection. "Andy? It's Jen. Your girlfriend just made me cry. Have you seen the pictures she took at the gala? Oh. My. God. They're fantastic. She's fantastic. So don't screw it up."

She disconnected.

"You guys are…" Shannon began, when her own phone rang. She connected.

"You're not going to hold Jen against me, are you?" asked Andy. "She was always the bossy big sister. Not my fault."

"Don't worry, Andy. But what a family. Doesn't anyone have a quiet personality?"

"No." Andy declared.

"No," Jen said simultaneously.

"I'm getting it in stereo again," Shannon said with a laugh. "Talk to you later."

Jen pointed at the sisters' picture. "Can you somehow make three more copies of that, so I can give it to my sisters as Christmas gifts? And I'll keep one, too. When framed, they'll be perfect."

Shannon hid her smile. How funny that the three sisters would be receiving her work for Christmas. And that two different family members had coincidently bought them.

"Sure. I've got the negative and I'll work it up for you. If you frame them here, I can give you a discount, but it's still a bit steep. Feel free to go elsewhere. It's okay. No hard feelings."

"No," said Jen. "You're the one with the eagle eye. I need your talent."

She gathered her purse and the folder of pictures. "I was concerned at first that Andy seemed to be plunging into a new relationship very quickly, but I'm beginning to understand why he's so smitten! I've never seen him as happy as he was on the dance floor Saturday night.

"My one concern—please— is that my little brother has the biggest heart of us all. And I'm praying it doesn't get broken. If you're as happy as he is, then I really hope it works out—for you both."

Shannon heard the warning—and worry—beneath the pretty words. "I've had a rocky road, too, and now I'm feeling my way, trying to smoothen it out. So do me a favor, Jennifer. From now on, if you want progress reports, ask your little brother."

To her amazement, Jennifer laughed. "Oh, I like you. You'd fit right in with us. You're feisty!"

Andy had said something similar about her. Funny, she didn't feel very feisty. Now that was something to think about. She and Matt had been a team, in theory, but with him away so much, that team often felt like an individual sport. Together they were strong. Like Andy's siblings and their spouses seemed to be. And when she and Matt were apart? She had to be strong, too.

Jennifer reached into her purse and pulled out a business card. Fidelity Investments. "When the pictures are ready for framing, just call me."

"Very impressive workplace," said Shannon. "High finance for you, and a teeny, tiny budget for me. Both ends of the spectrum."

"It's not my money I'm handling," said Jen. "I help folks plan and save for the future." She gave Shannon a meaningful look from under her lashes. "I have a sharp point on my pencil for budgets and saving too, so…."

Shannon chuckled. "I don't have enough coming in to consider a savings plan. What's left from my earnings, plus Matt's pension minus daycare and mortgage, just covers our needs. Period."

"I hear you, but you need to start saving now," said Jen. "Think about it." She waved and left the store.

Strong women? Probably. But if Jen was an indication, they sure butted into everyone else's business.

##

She looked forward to Andy's phone calls and texts, so when Shannon hadn't heard from him on Saturday, she began to wonder. Grocery and gift shopping distracted her, in addition to chatting with her mom and playing with Maddie.

Saturday night rolled in, quiet and…lonely. She stared at her phone. Not even a text. Maybe he was out with his friends at a club. They had to be single, too, so where else would they be on a Saturday night? If not that, maybe a card game? Gambling? Old college friends, he'd said, but not all pro ball players. He wouldn't encourage a high stakes game and take advantage of them. He played fair. She put the phone aside and found a movie to watch. She wasn't chasing him on a Saturday night.

On Sunday, she dropped Maddie off with Grandma and Grandpa for the afternoon and went into the gallery. She'd promised to work Sundays during the holiday season and didn't want to let Heather and Lynn down. Today they had advertised an afternoon soiree in honor of a visiting artist they were promoting.

Small glasses of champagne and a variety of cookies stood invitingly on offer at several tables throughout the gallery. Tasteful decorations in silver, white and blue provided a festive atmosphere. The focus of the gallery, of course, was on the artwork and the guest artist.

Shannon made her way through small groups, chatting and answering questions, introducing the clientele to the special guest artist. She had no photos to display herself because she'd offered Andy the "hands" picture from the aquarium's touch tank. She really had to make time for her own art. Maybe if the day held forty-eight hours...?

Busy preparing a purchase order for a customer, she only sensed someone standing near her desk. "Be right with you," she said, barely looking up.

"Take your time, Blue Eyes."

"Andy!" She jumped up and held out her hands. His green eyes gleamed and his smile was irresistible. "What are you doing here?"

"Checking out the art?" He winked and left her to her work as he blended with the visitors.

The minutes crawled for Shannon now. Talk about a surprise! A good one.

She found him studying a serigraph by Leroy Neiman. Not the renderings of athletes he was known for, but a carousel. A delightful compilation of yellow, purple and white horses, some with hoofs up, some hoofs down, but all looking ready to ride away and have fun.

"Maddie would love this," he said. "She'd want to get up there and ride."

"Before or after she threw a ball or block and cracked the glass or chipped the frame?" asked Shannon, with a wry grin. "But very thoughtful of you, Andy. And only four-grand to boot. Stick with prints for kids' rooms. Twenty bucks can go far."

"Man, you're taking the fun out of it," he teased. "So, can we leave yet?"

"We? You and I?" she asked pointing at him and herself.

"Is there anyone else I should know about?" he asked, looking over her shoulder.

"You flew back just to see me?"

"I'm keeping our weekly date."

Gobsmacked. Her mouth opened and closed. No words came.

"There are direct flights, you know." The guy looked so innocent. "In fact, there are direct flights almost everywhere I go." His words slowed down. "Most trips are under three hours."

It took a minute for her to connect the dots. "Not like to the Middle East. Is that what you're saying?"

"I fly to the game, and a couple of days later, I fly back. I've been doing it for years, and there's no reason to think that will change."

"I guess baseball is not a war," she mused. "It's only a little contest."

"Comparatively speaking, yes. But baseball gives the troops a mental break. Even in Afghanistan, they follow their teams." He took her hand. "It's a taste of home, Shannon."

"Matt called it the All-American game that every kid can play, rich or poor."

"He was right. And smart."

"And he was a big Red Sox fan."

"Natch," said Andy casually. "He was from Massachusetts, right? It's Boston or nothing. If he'd lived in Connecticut, he might have chosen the Yankees. And that – is a definite no-no."

She cracked up. Not just his words, but the way he said them, so dead-pan, but his eyes rolled. "Oh, Andy. I think Matt would have liked you."

His shenanigans stopped; his body stilled. "And that's the best compliment you could pay me. Thank you. I hope I never let him down. Or you."

"Thanks for helping out," said Shannon as she and Andy left the gallery.

"Handy-Andy, that's me. I can move boxes with the best of them," joked the man, as he led her to his vehicle in the parking lot and opened the passenger door. "With an ulterior motive to have some time alone before you pick up Maddie."

She flinched. He was playing by her rules, and she couldn't complain. But was she being stubborn about keeping him away from the baby? Or was her original idea the right one?

"And I know the perfect place for a quiet Italian dinner," he said once they were rolling. "More than pizza."

"You're being very mysterious," she said, noting the direction he was taking. Not to the North End, but closer to the harbor area, not too far from the aquarium.

"I'm just full of surprises." He pulled into a garage, led her to an elevator and pressed the top floor. PH. Penthouse.

"Welcome to my personal space, also known as my home."

She gulped. "You were right. This girl is surprised. Penthouse? I'm definitely in over my head."

"Nah. Don't let labels scare you. I bought it when Brian was traded to Houston a number of years ago. We'd been sharing a place near Fenway and I…I guess changes were in order. This place happened to be available, and I liked the view."

The elevator arrived, and he led her inside. Immediately, she took in the large scale and flow of the rooms. The brick wall. "It's a loft conversion, isn't it?" she said, walking through the hallway, living room and dining room combination. "Not at all what I was visualizing a penthouse to be. This is beautiful."

"Thanks. And yes, it's a conversion. I'll give you a tour later. Let's eat!"

"The stomach always rules," she said with a smile. "Lead on."

The airy kitchen contained everything a person would need to cook simple meals or complex ones. Shannon marveled at the double ovens, large fridge, built-in microwave. She walked around the room. "Smart placement. It looks so big, but everything's within easy reach."

"Right now, I'm reaching for our dinner," said Andy. "You sit down and relax. You've worked all day." He opened the refrigerator.

"And you've been on the go, too. Let me help." She took some loaded paper bags and containers from him and placed them on the counter.

"Plates are in there," he said, pointing at a cabinet. "Set the table and leave the rest to me."

Efficiency in motion. The man knew his way around a kitchen, and actually was humming under his breath as he worked. Soon the aroma of garlic and pasta sauce flavored the air. Her stomach rumbled as she laid the plates and silverware down.

"I know you, Blue-Eyes. The way to your heart is through your tummy."

Her new nickname? He'd used it earlier, too. It took her all of two seconds to admit to herself that she liked it. Friendly, warm but not too possessive. "If you were as hungry as I …"

An answering rumble came from his midsection. "I guess I am!"

Laughter came simultaneously, as did their steps toward each other.

He cupped her face in his hands, leaned in for a kiss. "You're finally here. I've been trying to figure out how to manage it."

"I suppose I don't have the freedom to come and go like most other women you've known."

His lips found hers again. "There are no others now, and the ones before came in a far second, or third or fourth," he murmured, while his mouth gently kept in contact with hers. Sweet little kisses.

She believed him. Every word. Her heart raced at the implication. "But it's only been a couple of weeks, Andy…" And she couldn't afford a mistake.

"Has it? I'm not keeping track. Mike fell for Lisa as soon as she opened the front door to him. They were both eighteen, but one look and bingo! He was a gone puppy.

"Throw out the rules and regs, Shan. They might apply at a game, but they don't apply to everything in life."

Her mind spun with new ideas, new impressions, and old memories. Had it only been a couple of weeks or had she known him for years? He was a whirlwind, yet he'd held back. Kisses came easily for them both; dancing together had been wonderful. And this surprise visit…? More cautious than he for sure, but slowly, she understood and smiled.

"So you're saying I should throw out the rules and regs regarding relationships?" she asked.

"Exactly. You're smart as well as talented. Have a little faith. Now, eat up."

##

After dinner, he took her for a tour, starting with a picture on his kitchen wall. "Brian has the same one of my folks. Actually, I think we all do. Lisa must have made copies."

Shannon recognized it from the programs. A happy-looking couple, so young and carefree in the snapshot.

"Meet Robert and Grace Delaney," he said, "but everyone called him Robbie."

"Those green eyes..." she murmured.

"Yeah. The acorns didn't fall far from that particular tree. He was the best dad. Signed us up for Little League the year before the...uh...accident. Always said Brian had the arm and I had the eye." He shrugged. "Maybe he was right or maybe we just believed him."

His voice had deepened and faded out. His eyes looked bleak. Easy to see how the loss still affected him. "And then there were five," he said, echoing his own words when he'd explained his uniform number. ""But thank goodness, we also had Mike. Without him...I don't know if Lisa could have managed."

"Lisa probably had the lion's share anyway."

His gaze jumped back to her.

"Wasn't Mike away a lot with the team?" Shannon asked. "I know he brought home a couple of Superbowl wins, and that must have taken a load of time and energy."

"But he never ignored us. We needed him, not only Brian and me, but the girls, too. Jen ran to her friends after the accident. I remember Mike going out looking for her on several nights afterwards. I remember Emily throwing up and Mike holding her over the sink."

And to think she worried about only one child. "Lisa and Mike should get the parents-of-the-century award. Look how great you all turned out."

"A shocker! But I'm glad you think so," said Andy, pressing her hand. "I guess we are a pretty happy bunch now."

"I agree, especially at a party." She smiled and asked, "How come I didn't really know all this in high school?"

A thoughtful, amused expression crept across his face. "Ever notice how self-centered teenagers are? You probably did know about Brian and me but focused on the newspaper and your own interests. Most other kids wanted to talk about the Riders, their chances and if we had any extra tickets to home games. Not about our home life." He paused, but his smile remained. "That's the way it works. The world's a stage, right? And kids are the stars in their own plays—or lives."

He led her to the big living room. A navy-blue upholstered couch, a traditional oak coffee table. And walls featuring landscapes, cityscapes and seascapes. All outdoors.

She stepped back and studied them. An oil painting, a serigraph, a watercolor, several framed photographs. "Lovely, each one." She went to his window and waved at the harbor. "Not enough natural beauty for you out there?"

"Love the view," he said, stretching his arm to her. "Come back and I'll guide you through my art."

"That landscape," he began, with a nod at the center work. "That's near where I was born, in the rural, western part of the state. And that one of the seashore…well, that's near the house on the Cape that Mike bought and where we spent some summers. And that skyline over there? I bet you can identify that place."

"I can. It's Boston."

"Look over there on the short wall."

"Fenway Park! Oh, my goodness. You're surrounded by your biography!"

She stepped back to see him more clearly. "You are amazing. This is so unique. So creative and most important...so meaningful. All these specific places...." Shaking her head, she kept looking from one painting to another.

"It's funny how it happened," he said. "I didn't plan it. After I bought this place with all the bare walls, I came across that familiar-looking landscape. I'm no art critic, but it appealed to me. So I bought it. Then I stumbled upon the beach picture, and I liked that one too."

"You did the right thing, Andy. You should always choose what makes you happy."

"I couldn't have said it better myself." He sealed his statement with another kiss, a long one. "Time to go," he whispered. "You have a little girl to pick up."

She glanced at her watch. "Oh, man. I totally lost track of the time."

CHAPTER TEN

If she could give good advice to Andy, why didn't she follow it herself? *Choose what makes you happy.* No doubt about Andy making her happy. So why did she hesitate in allowing him fully—one hundred percent—into her heart? Ninety-nine percent missed the mark.

Shannon was headed to the gallery on Tuesday, driving on autopilot. When she'd picked Maddie up at her parents' house on Sunday night, they'd expected Andy to be with her and were disappointed. More so after she mentioned his plans to fly back to Florida two days later, which meant this afternoon. Fortunately, Maddie had been distracted by her cousins and her mom's arrival and didn't react to the sound of his name.

Think! What was wrong with her? Matt's image inserted itself into her mind's eye. Matt! Her heart panged. Three years and still…. He'd want her to move on, she knew that. And she wasn't being fair to Andy.

Maybe she, herself, was the one who needed a therapist. Or maybe just someone to talk to who'd been there.

Any one of the Delaney siblings would do. They'd certainly known loss, but she immediately crossed them off her list. Deep in thought, she parked the car and started walking to the gallery in the cold air of mid-December. Snow was forecasted for that evening, promising a white Christmas this year. She hoped that didn't mean Christmas day, when she'd be driving to her in-laws.

As soon as she entered the gallery, she relaxed. This was her comfort zone, surrounded by an artist's vision, many times over. New paintings had come in and she catalogued the information, the artists' biographies, and took photos to document the pieces. Heather worked with her, calling collectors to inform them of the new inventory. A beautiful business, but definitely a business with an eye to profit and loss.

When her stomach rumbled, she laughed, checked the time and thought of the evening at Andy's place. A hungry couple.

"There she is!" The statement was followed by an indistinct babble.

Shannon turned at the familiar voices, and her eyes widened as Mike Brennan, Jennifer and Emily walked into the gallery. Mike was carrying the photo he'd bought. Shannon recognized the wrapping.

"Hey there," she said, stepping forward and glancing at the picture. "Nice to see you, but is something wrong?"

"Nope," he said. "Just changed my mind about waiting. I'd like it framed before I give it to Lisa. And since I know nothing about it, I brought these two along."

"We are know-nothings, too," said Emily. "But at least I'd know what I don't like." She paused. "Oh, wow. We really should know what Lisa wouldn't like."

"That's why we have Shannon," said Jen. "She'll know."

"I think I'm watching a sit-com with you guys," said Shannon, smiling at each of them. "I never know what to expect when you're all together. But come on back here where we handle framing, and let's take another look at *Wisdom.*"

A minute later, Mike unwrapped the photo and laid it on the table. Quiet descended as they all studied it.

"Oh, Mike...she's going to love it," said Emily. The petite woman took the man's arm and hugged it. "It's perfect."

"I know nothing about art," said Jen slowly, "but this...it's hitting me right here." She patted her chest. "This is a touchdown, Mike."

"Andy liked it, too, when he saw it," said Shannon quietly.

Heather's voice joined the group's. "We wanted Shannon to exhibit another piece, but she'd promised her next one to ...a friend."

In unison, the three visitors turned to Heather, then Shannon.

"Is she saying this is your work, Shannon?" Mike took the lead. "You're the artist? Or the photographer? Or whatever?"

Embarrassment heated her face, but pride filled her too. She was much more comfortable behind the camera than in front.

She nodded. "Yes. I have a small darkroom in my basement. Andy saw it a couple of times." She smiled at the memories. Her "etchings."

"And is he the friend Heather mentioned who has dibs on your next piece?" asked Jen.

Shannon nodded. "But I haven't given it to him yet."

"Man, I'd love to see it," said Emily.

"Then we'll have to crash his gorgeous pad after it's hung up," said Jen. "Shannon, this is a big deal. It's wonderful. Are you sure I can't help you stretch your budget to include more art supplies or babysitters or whatever you need?"

Shannon's gaze went from one to the other. She felt their praise, support, and friendship, and appreciated that their hearts seemed to be opening to her. Yet all she could think of was Andy—and the disquieting thoughts that had plagued her earlier.

Impetuously, she clasped Jen's hand and looked at Emily. "Does it ever get any easier?" she asked in a raspy voice. "That empty spot where someone once resided? The remembrances….? They catch me unaware at times, and block me from moving on."

"Oh, dear…Shannon," said Jen. "You're struggling. But I'll say yes, it does get easier, although the ache is still there, even after more than twenty years."

"The surprise memories are normal," said Emily. "They pop into my brain at the oddest times, when I least expect them."

"But without reaching for the touchdowns," added Mike, "you've got nothing to live for."

"Huh?"

"He means home runs, a fabulous catch, an unparalleled performance," said Emily quietly. "He means figuring out a way to move forward and find joy. Even though it's laughter through tears sometimes."

"We're honoring them by establishing the foundation, aren't we?" said Jennifer.

"In my family," said Heather, "when we raise a glass of wine, we say *l'chaim.* Which means, 'to life.'

What I've learned is to honor the past, embrace the present, and trust that the future will take care of itself."

"Heather! Not you, too." Her boss had become a friend, but obviously not close enough to reveal all the bits and pieces.

"No exemptions in this world, Shannon. You just have to deal. So, people! Are we now ready to frame this beautiful vision?"

The poignancy departed and the framing activity prevailed. Had this little unexpected support group provided her with instant therapy? Whatever the label, it was certainly a step in the right direction.

##

"Miss me?"

Shannon grabbed an afghan and tucked it around herself on the couch while she held her phone. "When are you coming home? Although I don't blame you if you hesitate. It's like a frozen tundra up here."

"I'll take that as a yes. So what if it's cold? You'll warm me up. Right?"

His voice—the warmth, the jocular tone— lifted her spirits. "I can't even warm myself up. I'm in long-sleeve sweats cuddled under a blanket, and I'm still shivering. It's been in the teens for too many consecutive days now. Even the walls are cold. Not kidding."

"I don't like the sound of that. Is your oil tank full enough? Do you have wood for your fireplace? Is Maddie's bedroom warm?"

His humorous tone had disappeared. This Andy was all business.

"Last year was mild," she said. "And no, I don't have any wood, but I have a portable heater I can use."

"Forget it," he said. "Too dangerous. I'll have a cord of wood sent over."

"No, you won't! I'll handle it."

"Consider it my Christmas gift, okay?"

She burst out laughing. "Not very romantic, but okay."

"Not romantic? Think about a roaring fireplace, two glasses of wine and a cushiony sofa. Seems pretty romantic to me. We can experiment when I get back."

The picture he created drew her in. She imagined them relaxing together, snuggling close. Andy's arm around her. "We sure can. I'm with you on experimenting. So, when are you coming home?"

"That's the second time you've used that word. Sounds really good."

Home. More than Boston. More than his own family. "The idea is growing on me, too."

"Keep it growing, Shannon. This isn't a practice run for me. So...how's Maddie? Are you laughing or crying?"

Although his question was amusing, his genuine interest came through. His connection to her daughter had weighed heavily on her mind, almost as important as her own relationship to Andy. The man deserved an answer.

"You can see for yourself when you get back."

"Well...how about that? You've made my day," he said. "My patience paid off, like when I'm at bat waiting for the perfect pitch. What made you reconsider?"

"I guess," she began slowly, "I'm beginning to trust again."

"Me?"

"I've trusted you from the start, Andy," she said. "It's me. It's life. I was afraid of more emotional setbacks. But Heather Greenburg said something that made an impression on me. She said, 'Embrace the present and trust the future to unfold.' I think she made a valid point. I had to get out of my own head and open my mind."

"It seems I missed an important conversation."

"Don't worry," she replied, her tone light. "Your family covered for you. Mike, Jen and Emily were there. But you, Andrew Delaney, are the beneficiary of that important conversation. It was so easy for me to give advice to my mother-in-law, when I really needed some advice myself."

"You were ready to listen, Shan. But I wouldn't let my guard down with her if I were you."

"I'm hoping for the best. It's Christmas. Good things can happen."

"Love you, Shan."

She gulped. The L word? "Do you realize what you just said?" she asked softly.

"I believe it was something like, 'see you Saturday at your place.' I'll bring dinner."

She laughed. "Good try, but that wasn't it. And regarding dinner, I'll cook for you."

##

Andy had plans. He'd put his Miami condo on the market and buy something in Ft. Myers, near JetBlue Park. He usually stayed in a hotel for the six weeks of spring training, but having their own place made more sense, especially with a child.

He checked the time and stared out the plane window, impatient for the flight to land. A new sensation. Normally he took things in stride, was known for having a 'good head on his shoulders.' Nope, never this impatient, not even when flying to a World Series game, where he'd been honored to help the Sox win twice. But being with Shannon was different. Even more special. He checked his watch again. Had the hands even moved?

The cold air hit him savagely and stole his breath as soon as he left the airport. Shannon hadn't been kidding about the plunging temperature. He took a cab to his place, checked the mail, grabbed a heavy parka and woolen ski hat from his closet and set out again. Shopping first. A six-pack of beer, a bottle of pinot grigio—Shannon's favorite—and a Boston cream pie would do it. Oh, maybe Maddie would like that big cookie with the colorful sprinkles on top. He got behind the wheel again, glad that the entire evening waited. Only five o'clock and he was on his way.

He pulled into her driveway and noted the wood stacked ten feet from the house. Excellent. Maybe that fireplace would get used later.

After grabbing his packages, he got out of the car and looked up. And there she was. More beautiful than ever, in jeans and a navy sweater, with her hair loosely tied behind her neck. Shannon's open arms and welcome home kiss was everything he could have asked for.

When he stepped into the entryway, he was greeted by delicious smells and the sight of Maddie on the floor, thoroughly engrossed in very vocal play with her toy farm.

"It smells delicious in here," Andy said, before turning his attention to the toddler. "Hey, Maddie! What have you got there?"

He lowered himself to the floor next to the little girl as she turned to gaze up at him. "Moo-o-o!" she said, holding up a miniature plastic cow for his inspection. "Andee! See my cow?"

"I do! And who's this guy over here?"

"Piggy!" and then she was off and running, pointing out her various play friends. "Dis my horsie, dis da farmer. And my sheep!"

Smiling and delighted, he scooped her into his arms. "Ah, Maddie. I've missed you! Very, very much! And guess what? I brought you a surprise for after dinner, if Mommy says it's okay."

"What?" Maddie asked. He glanced at Shannon, gesturing toward the cookie he'd brought and silently requesting permission to show it to the little girl. "This is for later," he said, walking over to the counter, still carrying Maddie so he could point out the intriguing package. "What do you think?"

"Yummy!" She pronounced enthusiastically after checking out the treat. "Cookie for later!"

She turned in his arms, looked up at him expectantly and allowed him to hold her tight. Such a familiar position for a favorite uncle who adored his nieces and nephews.

"Let's do something fun. Let's sing a song, Mommy can join in, too." The child looked for Shannon, who was wiping her eyes.

"Row, row, row your boat, Gently down the stream…" he began, as he set Maddie back down on the floor.

A family kitchen, with delicious aromas and sounds of song and fun, was a familiar, comfortable setting for him, even though more than twenty years had passed.

He glanced at Shannon and smiled indulgently. "I love being here at home with you and Maddie, babe. I really do. But you've got to stop crying!"

"They're happy tears, Andy. The best kind."

He whispered to Maddie, "Your mommy needs some kisses from us."

"Ok!" She threw herself at her mom. Andy steadied Shannon from the impact and kissed her the way his special woman should be kissed.

"Bedtime's coming soon," he whispered.

"It certainly is." Her warm and promising smile mesmerized him in the same way a hypnotist mesmerized an audience.

##

Maddie fell asleep surprisingly quickly, probably exhausted from all the excitement of the special dinner and treats and extra playtime. Shannon gave her daughter one last kiss and returned to the living room. A small, decorated tree stood in the corner, while Santa and his elves paraded across the mantel. Andy was peering up the fireplace chimney, opening and closing a lever.

"Making it nice and safe for Santa?" she joked. "Truth is, I've never checked the damper. Thanks for not filling the house with smoke and embers."

"Of course," he said, glancing at her. "Baseball's not my only talent." His grin set her to laughing, and she knelt next to him. "I'm counting on that."

"Good." He reached for the log holder and selected a few pieces from the pile he'd just brought in, then laid them on the grate, put kindling on top and tucked crumpled newspapers around everything. Lighting a long match, he nurtured a small fire until it burned sure and steady.

"Every New Englander should master the art of fire-building," he said, turning his head toward her.

"Sorry, but I never learned."

"Next time, I'll coach you." He closed the mesh fireplace screen, stood and offered his hand. She clasped it, strong and firm, and easily rose next to him.

"A fire always looks so inviting," she said. "I brought the rest of the wine in." She nodded at the bottle and glasses set on the coffee table. "But I don't think I'd light a fire for just Maddie and me. If my back were turned, she could get into trouble."

"Point taken. And if your electricity goes out during a storm, and your furnace doesn't work? What then?"

"Curse myself for not having a backup generator?"

"Nope. You build a fire! Put Maddie in her high chair while you work."

They sat on the sofa, and Shannon reached for the wine. "The man has answers for everything."

"I wish I had all the right answers, but nope. Just trying to figure it out as I go along. Like you do."

She felt his arm around her, pulling her close. Exactly where she wanted to be. "This is nice," she said quietly. "Want some music?"

A sweet tenor voice sang to her about chestnuts and Jack Frost. She should have guessed he could carry a tune.

"And he sings, too," she whispered.

"I have many talents." He leaned closer and lightly tasted her lips.

She'd been waiting, wanting and...worrying. But now she forgot about every distraction except Andy Delaney and the flame he was igniting in her. She hadn't gone out searching, but a wonderful second love seemed to have found her. Still...

"It's been a very long time for me, Andy. So I'm a bit...umm...nervous...."

His light breath in her ear made her shiver. "Oh! So good...I'd almost forgotten..."

"Then I'll remind you." His lips traveled down her neck to her collarbone while his hand found the hem of her sweater and tunneled beneath. His fingertips danced on her bare skin. She gasped as he climbed slowly higher, her body tightening, her breasts so in need of him. Such need...and then...nothing.

"You call the shots," he said, his voice tight. "I don't want to screw this up and risk everything we've found together."

She pushed his hand higher. "Sweet, but open the clasp. Now!"

"My pleasure," he murmured while unlocking the front hook of her bra. Her breast filled his hand. Gently he traced around the sides, then again, climbing higher toward the sensitive center. He heard her gasps, felt her shivers. Her nipple budded as soon as he touched it. He leaned closer and made love to it with his tongue.

Her arms tightened around him. "Oh. My. God. So good, Andy, so good."

Andy could have cheered. Not because of any special love-making prowess he'd offered, but because Shannon's heart wasn't confused. In the throes of intimacy, she'd called *his* name. Poor Matt was not there with them.

"Let me see you, touch you," she whispered, opening several buttons on his shirt.

"I'm all yours." He inhaled and focused on her touch, enjoying the sensation of her fingers as they trailed across his chest, across his nipples. She paused in the place over his heart.

"It's strong and steady," she murmured. "Like you."

Her words meant everything. He wrapped her in his arms, and somehow the sofa cushions fell to the floor. They fell on top of them while the fire provided a constant glow. Skin to skin, they twined and danced, he in the lead, then she, exploring each other in the most intimate and infinite of ways. From mouth to thigh, caressing, stroking, the heat building, the tension rising and rising until—

"Now, Andy. Now!"

He entered her and prayed her name.

And when they were able to breathe again, she rolled toward him, caressing his face, gently kissing his mouth. "We'll call it the Fireplace Symphony because…be-cause…" Her tears fell.

"Yeah," he said. "As beautiful as any piece of music ever written. I knew it would be."

"You did?"

"I fell in love with you almost immediately." He tapped her nose. "And you didn't make it easy. Thank God for that auction."

She began to giggle. "Came in handy, huh?"

"All's fair in love and war, as they say. Anyone so precious is worth fighting for. And I'm fighting, Shan. Memories. In-laws. A cute kid. A military hero."

He became silent for a moment, his brow creased. "I'm just a baseball player, Shannon, who's trying to make the greatest catch of his life."

She stroked his cheek. "Millions of fans adore you, and you're just a baseball player?" she repeated, shaking her head. "And that's why I love you, Andrew Delaney. Not too big for your britches." She opened her arms. "Let's catch each other and make a home."

"The best idea I've ever heard. I love you, Shan." He took her in his arms and kissed her with promise, until reality set in. "We'll have to start in the new year. Our first Christmas together…and we'll be apart. Crazy, but with your commitment to the Roberts's, it can't be helped."

"You're right about this year. I guess we'll be creating our own roadmap as we go along, potholes included."

CHAPTER ELEVEN

"You're looking happy, Shannon," said her mom the next morning. "With Andy joining us, we'll have a full house tonight—but I'm not cooking. We'll pick up some lasagnas in the North End." She reached for Maddie. "Want to help me bake cookies today? That much I can do."

"I'm glad this is my last Sunday at the gallery, Mom. We'll both have more down time now." Helen was part of the family business and put in as many hours as needed. "I'll bring salad ingredients for tonight."

Maddie's eyes stayed on Grandma. "Cookies! Make cookies! I roll dough, Grandma." She mimicked the action. "I do it."

Precious child. So bright-eyed and happy that Shannon shivered in surprise when a frisson of concern swept through her. She and Maddie were strong and steady now. Why change things? Why rock the boat?

But was strong and steady enough? Now her stomach twisted. At one time it had been. But now it wasn't. She wanted Andy in her life as well.

"Maddie learned a new song," she said. "Want to sing it for Grandma?"

"*Row, row, row your boat...* "

Shannon and her mom joined in and Maddie beamed. "An-dee taught me. Again! *Row, row...* "

Shannon left for work with the sound of Jingle Bells in the air and had no time to either second-guess herself or to indulge in daydreams from the moment she stepped into the gallery. Browsers turned into customers who needed help; follow-up phone calls had to be made while inquiries had to be answered and orders had to be packaged. The day sped by, but she was late leaving that afternoon and the last to arrive at her parents' place after stopping at the supermarket. Almost breathless, she felt herself relax when she spotted Andy's vehicle.

She relaxed even more when she saw him holding Maddie on his shoulder. Her daughter was in heaven.

"Look who just walked in, Maddie," he said, his eyes locking with hers.

"Hi," she said, as if they were alone in the room. He came towards her, lowering Maddie to his chest, and Shannon knew what he'd do before he leaned in. The kiss was personal, possessive and wonderful.

"Staking your claim?" she asked.

"You bet I am. Right, Maddie?"

Maddie reached for her mom. "Kisses."

"Are we uh…spilling the beans?" asked Andy softly, nodding at the entire Murphy gathering. "Might be a good time."

"If we can seize the right moment," said Shannon. "Sounds like everyone is pretty chatty today."

As they sat at the dinner table a little while later, Shannon's brother-in-law, Steven, clinked his glass for attention. He and her sister, Amy, were simply the cutest couple in the world.

"Amy and I have some good news," he said.

Amazing how an entire gathering of people could straighten their posture simultaneously. Her mom's hand went to her neck. Her dad was totally focused. Shannon had the same inkling they all had.

Amy piped up. "We're pregnant. Three months. And we're thrilled!"

Shannon caught Andy's eye and shook her head. Now wasn't the right time. She didn't want to steal her sister's limelight. Andy nodded, as though reading her mind.

"Congratulations! So exciting." She rose and went to kiss Amy and Steven. "I'm so happy for you both. Another baby to love—and spoil—in this family."

She saw Andy take in the scene. His eyes glistened as he watched and nodded. The corners of his mouth turned upward. She knew what he was thinking and picturing as he projected Shannon and himself into that situation. The guy was jumping ahead too quickly for her!

Daniel got her attention. "Are you still planning on that drive to your in-laws next Saturday? It's a crappy idea, if you ask me. Christmas Day, just you and Maddie for a hundred miles. And the weather forecast includes a chance of snow by the end of the week. Tell them to come here instead."

"Wish I could, but I promised," she said quietly. "It's...ah...difficult."

"It is a crappy idea," echoed Andy. "So how about I drive and drop you and Maddie off at their house? Consider me your Uber. I don't even have to say hello to them. I'll spend the night with Mike's parents in Woodhaven, where I grew up. It's only a couple of exits from Amherst. Mike's brother and family will be there, too. But Mike and Lisa are staying in town with Jen and Doug, his sister and parents." He brushed his hands together. "Always logistics, but problem solved."

Words of approval came from all around. Her family's relief was palpable.

"Did you just come up with this driving idea?" Shannon asked.

"Nah. I've been trying to figure out how to convince you." His gaze moved around the table, and his quick grin appeared. "I didn't know I'd have an army to back me up."

Shannon tried for an early Christmas Eve. She tried for a short visit to both her mom's place and Andy's sister's house. Somehow, the goodbyes took forever each time, but worth Maddie's cranky tears when they finally left Mike and Lisa's.

"So, tots need their sleep," said Andy after Maddie quieted down to the rocking of the car.

"So do mommies," replied Shannon with a yawn, "especially if we want an early start. I promised the Robertses we'd arrive around noon."

"Do they know I'm driving you?"

"They're aware that a friend is driving me," she said. "That's all they need to know for now. They'll see soon enough that you're not a girlfriend."

He chuckled in that delightful tenor voice, and she joined in, adding, "Minimal disclosure saves a lot of aggravation."

"Sounds familiar. Brian's wife believes in that philosophy, too."

"I really hit it off with Megan at the gala," said Shannon. "I liked her a lot."

"Well…let's see…your late husband was a hero, and her ex was and is a scumbag, now rotting in prison."

"Geez," said Shannon, turning towards him, eyes wide. "What do you mean?"

"Alcoholic, gambler and all-around scuzzball. Left Megan when Josh was six months old. Actually, Megan caught him with a woman and threw him out. So the question is, does her son really need to know the details?" A rhetorical question, which he answered himself. "Nope. And there you have it in a nutshell. Josh doesn't need to know—now. Words to live by."

"I totally agree. That kind of darkness would cloud his life."

"Josh is crazy about Brian. The boy was thirsting for a dad and wound up with the best. Nice and legal, too. Another layer of protection."

They arrived at her house, and Andy pulled into the driveway. When he lifted a sleeping Maddie from her car seat and Shannon gathered the rest of their stuff, she wondered about his revelations. His active mind had jumped ahead while she was absorbing and relishing one day at a time. But he was right to mention the dad thing. They'd need to talk.

##

A late start the next morning saw them on the road closer to eleven o'clock. Shannon had to admit that between the duffel bag of clothes, Maddie's toys, Christmas gifts and a bed rail, they'd filled up Andy's vehicle pretty well.

"Are we finally ready?" she asked as she locked her seatbelt.

"We?" asked Andy with a laugh. "I've been ready for hours."

"Yes…well…get used to it. No tight ships around here. But we try."

"You do great. Let's see if we can beat the snow."

The sky had turned a pale white with no sun to be seen. "I'll settle for a two-hour delayed arrival time," said Shannon. "Oops, make it three hours. I want you safely with Mike's folks before I can view the trip as done."

In a few minutes, they approached the Mass Pike, heading west, and Shannon leaned back to enjoy the ride. From the back seat, she could hear Maddie singing Jingle Bells and telling a story of what they were doing and where they were going.

"She never stops," said Shannon, shaking her head.

"Her vocabulary is growing unbelievably," said Andy. He called out, "Maddie, I have a new song for you."

"*Row, row your boat…*"

"This is a new one. Are you ready?"

"Maddie ready!"

"*Over the river and through the woods to grandmother's house we go…*"

Shannon joined in and for an hour, they kept it up while snow started falling. "Maybe you can sing it for Grandma Susan when we get there. But no more now. I need a break."

"Break?"

"A rest. My mouth needs to rest. Yours too. How about some quiet time for a while?" She handed Maddie a favorite book with colorful cardboard pages that looked dogeared.

"I read now. Ducky book."

"Wow. She can really keep you busy," said Andy. "Being a mom is—is—challenging."

"Yep. It's just plain hard, but so worth it." She eyed him sideways. "Having second thoughts?"

"Too late for that. Maddie's the greatest kid of all time. So don't think you can get rid of me that easily." He patted the left side of his chest. "Besides…she's sitting in here, right next to her mom."

Oh, yeah. She squeezed his thigh and his hand covered hers as they headed north out of Springfield toward Amherst.

"Another half-hour to go," said Shannon, "and the snow's starting to accumulate." She scanned the ground, sky and horizon, which was almost nonexistent. "I wish you could stay with us, but maybe a local hotel would work better than you going back to the Mass Pike."

"Do you see me worried?" asked Andy. "This vehicle is as steady as they come."

Until it hits a patch of black ice. But she didn't say anything, just appreciated his calm confidence behind the wheel. She gave him directions when he exited the highway, and soon they approached the residential neighborhood where Susan and John lived.

"I'll give them a heads-up to open the garage door," said Shannon, reaching for her phone. Not taking chances, she chose their landline number. Success!

"Look, Maddie," she said a minute later. "See Grandma and Grandpa waiting for us?"

Andy pulled into the driveway and drove as close to the garage door as possible. "Okay, gang. Let's do it."

Shannon got Maddie from her car seat while Andy unloaded the cargo area. Two trips into the garage with the paraphernalia before Shannon joined him inside with Maddie.

"Give her to me," said Susan, reaching for her granddaughter. "Finally, we get to see her again."

"It's been only three weeks, Susan," Shannon said lightly, trying to joke.

"Hello, there," Andy interrupted. He looked at the older couple. "Glad to be of help. Enjoy your visit." He turned to Shannon. "What time tomorrow?"

"Definitely while it's still daylight." She looked at her in-laws. "How about one o'clock? Will that work for you?"

"How about next week?" asked Susan.

"That's a grandma for you," said John, "always wanting more time." He stepped closer to his wife and reached for Maddie, who lifted her arms for a hug.

Shannon smiled. Maddie would be doted upon while Shannon counted down the hours to leave. "Thanks so much, Andy," she said, stepping close and pressing her hand in his.

"Got your cell?" he asked softly. "Call me anytime if you need to."

She nodded. "Bye now."

"Hang on a second," said John. "I thought you looked familiar. You're the baseball player, right?"

"That's my job, yes," he said, reaching out his hand to shake the other man's. "Andy Delaney."

"Well, isn't that something?" He looked from Andy to Shannon. "When you said a friend was driving you down…"

"A friend did drive me. Andy and I go back a long way."

"And I have a way to go," said Andy. "So, before the roads get worse, so long, everyone. Merry Christmas!" He walked toward the driveway and waved.

"An-dee! An-dee! Down, Grandpa, down." Shannon saw her father-in-law taken by surprise. Maddie twisted in his arms and got away. Running to Andy, she smashed into his legs and raised her arms.

He picked the child up and said, "Tomorrow, sweetheart. I'll see you right here again tomorrow."

Shannon took Maddie from him and whispered, "Just go. I'll distract her."

He nodded. "But this is the first and last time for this nonsense." He kissed Shannon quickly before leaving. As the garage door slowly closed, she heard the SUV's motor roar to life.

"Let's go inside where it's warm," said John, reaching for a bag.

"Great idea," said Shannon, still soothing Maddie. "Go to Grandma while I help with the stuff. I bet there's a beautiful Christmas tree inside."

"There certainly is. Want to see the tree, Maddie? Let's go see it and open some of your presents."

"We have gifts to add, too," said Shannon as they all entered the house.

Susan's hard glance told its own story, and Shannon sighed.

##

The framed picture of Maddie was an instant success. Susan oohed and ahhed and set it in the center of the mantel where everyone could see it.

"I've got my 35-millimeter with me today," said Shannon, "and I can take some shots of the three of you together." She couldn't think of a better activity. In front of tree, sitting on the sofa, Maddie in their arms, Maddie opening her gifts—enough for several children. Traditional-type pictures mixed with candid shots.

"It'll be fun to see what my darkroom produces," she said as she snapped her last picture, catching Maddie's delight in tearing off the paper wrappings and making a general mess. More fun than playing with the items inside!

Shannon glanced at her watch. "Seems like no nap today," she said. "I hope she stays happy for the rest of the afternoon."

Maddie busied herself flitting from new toy to new toy, and crinkling the wrapping, singing happily to herself.

"Over da riva and trew da woods to Grandmudder's house we go..."

Susan's eyes popped wide open, her mouth agape. "Wow, Maddie. You're fantastic. That's a pretty hard song for a little girl. Where did you learn it? In daycare?"

Maddie shook her head vehemently back and forth. "An-dee sing it. Andy and Mommy and me." She looked around. "Andy?"

Shannon knelt by her daughter's side. "Andy's coming tomorrow. And then we go home to Boston."

"Tomorrow?" She made a forward motion with her arm.

"Yes. Tomorrow. When you get up in the morning, it will be tomorrow."

She cocked her head, wrinkled her brow. "'kay." Then she reached for a new book, toddled over and handed it to John.

Her grandfather's smile crossed his entire face. "You want a story? Of course."

"Come with me," said Susan, leading Shannon to the kitchen, away from the two readers. "I must have my say before this goes any further."

Shannon braced herself.

"You need a life...okay, I get that a life includes men," Susan began, walking back and forth before facing Shannon. "But my son—your husband—was a hero, Shannon. He died a hero, fighting for his country. And now—now—you're choosing a man who—who plays ball?" Her arms gestured wildly. "This 'An-dee,' as Maddie calls him, played baseball while Matthew was fighting a war! While Matthew died. How can you…? How can you possibly compare Matthew with one of those *boys of summer,* as they're called?"

Her mother-in-law was breathless. Outraged. And totally irrational.

Shannon took a deep breath, her thoughts coming together, she hoped, in a way that made sense.

"Not all battles, Susan, take place in the open where we can see them. Hidden landmines explode everywhere, and they come in many forms." She inhaled deeply again. "Andy was hit by one of those hidden landmines when he lost both parents at nine years old." She paused. "Did you hear what I said? A nine-year-old child. A car accident—actually, not too far from here—and poof! They were gone. I'd say he's had more than a fair share of troubles in life. And managed to handle them."

She took Susan's hand. "I'm hoping you can absorb this, Susan. I've known Andrew Delaney for a long time. And I can tell you with full confidence that he is a wonderful man. A man I can trust."

Susan's glance sharpened. "Not better than Matt."

"Two brave men, Susan. Two honorable men. Let's just say that I don't know how I got so lucky twice in a lifetime."

Susan lips quivered, her eyes blinked quickly. "And our Maddie?" she asked, her voice shaking. "My Matthew's daughter? How will she know him?"

Tears pooled in Shannon's eyes. Were they finally coming to the crux of Susan's worries? "We'll tell her that she has two daddies. One in heaven. And one here on earth."

Silence reigned for a moment. "We'll tell her stories about Matt," said Susan, moving away from

137

Shannon and starting to pace. "Show her lots of pictures."

"Yes. Yes, we will." Shannon's breath hitched as she thought of her handsome and jovial husband. "He will not be forgotten, Susan. I can promise you that." As her daughter got older, little by little, she'd be able to understand.

"I think Maddie is lucky to have two sets of grandparents," said Shannon, "and I'd like to continue that way. But not at Andrew's expense, and not at Maddie's either." She stepped closer to Susan. "He loves us both, and we love him." She lowered her voice. "In the near future Andy, Maddie and I will become a family. And we sincerely hope that you and John will choose to be part of it—as much or as little as you want. I'm really hoping that everything will sort of fall into place." Patting Susan's hand, she left the room.

She'd given it her best shot, but producing miracles was beyond her paygrade—and her skills. Maybe they'd get lucky. If not world peace, then peace in the family. She glanced at the winter-white scene outside—the perfect time of the year for miracles.

CHAPTER TWELVE

Andy arrived at the Brennan's home in time for a drink before dinner. Warm greetings filled the air from Irene and Bill as well as Mike's brother, David, and his wife. Their two sons, attending Boston University, shook Andy's hand, but he wrapped them in hugs.

"Good to see you guys." He turned to Irene and handed her a bottle of good cabernet. "Thanks for making room for one more at the last minute."

"No thanks needed," she replied. "There's always a place at our table for you and the family and the extended family. Goodness, we've grown so much, it's hard to keep track of everyone!"

Despite the fully white hair and crinkles at the corner of her eyes, Irene seemed as sharp as ever. It was Bill, however, who raised his glass first. "Now that we're assembled, I toast to the happiness of the family and to the old folks' new adventure."

"I don't see any old folks around here!" said Andy, who watched and wondered.

"Always good to hear, Andrew," said Bill "But listen up, everyone! I'm selling the pharmacy and retiring. Got a fair offer from a national chain, and I took it. It's time to kick up our heels and have some fun!"

"Hear, hear! I second that," said David. "You've worked hard all your lives and deserve as much fun as you can get."

"And the first thing we're doing," said Irene, "is moving to Boston. I want to be near you and Mike and my grandchildren. There's no reason to stay out here anymore when we finally have time to—to play! I guess that's as good a word as any."

She pointed at the young men. "We can finally go to your games—in person, Andrew. Not just watch thirty-second videos from your dad's phone, David." She turned to Andy. "I can go to Briana's concerts and Bobby's games as well. And if Jennifer's children want us around, we'll go there, too. We'll take advantage of everything the town has to offer." Her grin stretched across her face. "Red Sox, here we come!"

"I'll supply the tickets," Andy said. "Good for you guys!"

Irene was in her own world, but a good one, all about time with her grandkids.

"You know, Andy," she said, "Speaking of Jen—I taught her how to quilt many years ago, and I can do the same for her girls—if they'd like it."

"Nice of you, but they're only five years old. I think you'd wind up with a lot of bloody fingers."

Bill chuckled. "She's getting ahead of herself. But she's speaking for both of us. I want to be closer, too."

So that's the way it was with grandparents. No downside for them or the children. He hoped Shannon's in-laws would come around—for all their sakes. He wondered what was happening in Amherst right now and checked his pocket for his phone. He'd be calling her soon.

Walking to the big living room window, he looked across Hawthorne Street at his boyhood home. Young boyhood, he amended. From age four to nine. Five years. He'd been old enough for memories.

"Who lives there now?" he asked aloud, when he heard light footsteps approaching.

"I don't really know," said Irene. "A working couple. The house has turned over three times, but we can't bring ourselves to get very friendly. Can't see us going in and out the front door like we used to with Grace and Robbie." She sighed. "So many years, and yet"—she squeezed his arm—"Oh-h...I'm so ready to move to Boston."

He gave her a hug. "And Boston's waiting for you." But his mind was still on the house across the street. "See that front porch?" he asked, pointing at it.

"Of course," she replied.

"Right where it's always been," said Bill, who'd joined them.

"I was recently reminded that the front porch was where we voted," said Andy. "On a freezing cold night after the funeral, my sibs and I made the most important decision of our lives. Do we separate or stay together? Lisa gave us a choice."

"Believe me," said Irene quietly, "I know exactly how that vote went."

"No reason to look back, honey," said Bill. "It all worked out well in the end."

Andy sensed a crosscurrent of hidden meaning here. Something only the other two knew. He waited and was rewarded.

"The truth is, Andy, we thought it really would be best if you kids went to your relatives," said Irene. "I couldn't conceive how Mike and Lisa at such a young age, and with his career just starting, could take care of four children who were hurting so much. Full of grief and fear. Bill and I worried about Mike being distracted and getting injured. Money was tighter than today, too, and there were five of you he was taking on.

"I told Lisa I was trying to see it from all sides, to be a reasonable parent to everyone, but in the end, I couldn't be. I was Mike's mother. He was my first responsibility."

Instinct told him not to respond. To remain quiet and open his mind to the situation. "Lisa never said a word to us," he finally said.

Irene sighed. "She wouldn't because she didn't want to destroy the good relationship between you kids and us—your parents' closest friends. She took the high road. Oh, we put Lisa in a tough place, God forgive us, because we worried about Mike."

Lisa had been and still was smarter than any of them realized—except Mike. "I guess we all have memories that haunt us," said Andy. "I can understand how you were in a difficult position, especially since, without a will or directives, no one knew what my parents would have wanted. Fortunately, like Bill just said, everything turned out all right."

His thought raced. His sister must have been very upset, must have felt abandoned again. Instead of receiving support, the Brennans had withdrawn it. He felt a frisson of anger build and spun towards his hosts.

Worry lines showed on their brows, around their mouths. In their eyes, he saw an appeal for understanding. And he paused. Okay, so they weren't perfect. And they'd definitely had second thoughts about their attitude back then. He supposed they were simply human, with all the strengths and frailties that went along with that condition. Relationships—even when well- intentioned—could be delicate, complicated and full of conflict.

"Hard choices, impossible decisions," said Bill. "But parenting is never easy. Right, David?"

"If only...but we love it."

Andy's thoughts flew to Maddie. A joyful baby. What if he and Shannon had different ideas later on? Would she call the shots because he wasn't the "real" father? Other memories pierced his brain. Arguments between Lisa and Mike, especially when money flowed more freely, and he'd bought extravagant gifts for them. Lisa had been the legal guardian, but when he and Brian had questions about anything, they ran to Mike first.

"In the end," said Bill, "we came around, we took heart. Besides Mike and Lisa, all the branches of your family have become ours, too. Look at our family picture gallery over there." He waved his arm at a wall covered with framed photos. "Love always triumphs, Andrew. Always."

"If that's true, Bill, I've got no problems."

##

The next day Andy said his goodbyes and set off for the half-hour or so drive to get Shannon and Maddie. The snow had stopped the night before, but the sky was still overcast. His vehicle handled the snow-covered side streets, and fortunately, the main highways had been plowed.

He and Shannon had compared notes on the phone after everyone had retired to their own rooms, and they were hopeful that progress had been made.

"It would be really cool if Maddie liked baseball," he'd said. "What's the chance of that?"

"One hundred percent," was Shannon's quick reply. "When she sees you in uniform, and hears me cheering…? Are you kidding? She'll want to be right where the action is." He heard her sing *Take me Out to the Ball game* before she continued. "Besides, I really do like baseball. We'll make a party of it with my grandfather and whoever else wants to go. Maybe even Susan and John someday."

"Ahh—I wouldn't push it," he said. "But tuck the thought away for later."

"I guess you're right. It's just that I want everyone to be as happy as possible, and what better place to forget your troubles than inside a baseball park?"

"No argument there," he said with a laugh. "I've heard that many times before from lots of Sox fans. Maybe that's the only reason they come."

"Nah," said Shannon. "They want to see my world-famous power hitter smash one out of the park."

"There's that too," agreed Andy, still amused.

As he sat behind the wheel recalling their conversation, he was totally relaxed, totally looking forward to kissing her hello.

Which didn't happen. The garage door was open, and he walked inside to the house door just as it flew open. A tiny whirlwind greeted him with a babble of words, the sweetest one being *An-dee.*

"Hi, baby," he said, swinging her up in his arms. "Have you been a happy girl? A good girl for Mommy and Grandma? Did you get presents?"

"Yes! Yots a presents. And I sing da song."

"Wow! Will you show me later?" He glanced quickly at the woman who made his heart race and smiled.

"She's a one-person entertainment center, that girl," joked Shannon, her eyes devouring him. He adjusted his hold on Maddie and leaned down to kiss her mom.

"Seems like years," he whispered. "Are you ready to go?"

The door opened wider from inside, and Shannon's father-in-law appeared, saying, "Come on in for a minute before you take off."

He glanced at Shannon, who shrugged. "I've tried my best," she whispered.

"Be right there," Andy called, standing Maddie on the ground before taking off his work boots. "Don't want to mess up the floors."

"Maddie have boots, too!" announced the child. Then she twirled in a circle with her arms up.

He walked inside the kitchen with the rest, but they moved into the living room, where Mrs. Roberts waited.

Shannon began introductions, but the woman waved them away. "Sit. Sit down," she invited while she paced.

He followed Shannon's example and sat next to her on the sofa.

"I know things are changing," Susan Roberts began. "I can't say I'm thrilled, but I can't stop it either." She looked straight at Andy.

"My friends tell me," she continued, "that in-laws should keep their mouths shut and their wallets open if they want a good relationship with their children. But I'll fail on both counts. John and I certainly can't compete with your wallet, and I can't just step aside and be quiet."

He watched the woman pace with nervous energy, panting and stressed.

"There's no competition as far as I'm concerned," he said softly. "No one can compete with grandparents. They're special. So please sit down and catch your breath. I know CPR, but I'd hate to have to use it during our first real conversation."

As he watched, the woman actually cracked a smile. "Point taken." She found a chair. "I guess I'm looking for reassurance, even crumbs would do," she said. "So, teaching Maddie *Over the River to Grandma's House* was your idea?"

"I grew up singing with my family. We had a lot of fun. Old songs, new songs, and rounds like *Row, Row, Row Your Boat.*" He waited a moment. "My sisters, brother and I still sing, Mrs. Roberts. We think our folks would be happy to know that and more about what bonds us."

"Shannon told us what happened." She nodded and her eyes filled. "And my son? What does…"

"Our son," said John, interrupting her, "would be happy to know his daughter is in good hands." He walked to his wife and laid his palm on her shoulder.

"How he treats children has always been the measure of a man to me," John continued. "And I'm thinking that this man, sitting right here, can catch a child and hold on tight even more easily than a pop fly to the outfield."

Andy could say nothing after that endorsement. He walked to John and offered his hand. "Thank you for that. I won't let you down."

Turning to Shannon, he added, "Or you."

CHAPTER THIRTEEN

As if all the air had been sucked out of their lungs, neither Shannon nor Andy said much during the first hour on the road toward home. Maddie had fallen asleep, so no noise came from the backseat either.

"A lot to digest, huh?" asked Andy quietly.

"Almost too much. It was a good step forward, but there might be a backward turn too."

Andy shrugged. "We did our best, and at least John knew it. Susan may be the talker, but it looks to me as if he's the spine that keeps them grounded. Time to move on, Shan."

"I totally agree. So much ahead of us. What did you have in mind?"

He flashed a sideways grin. "You are just too easy, my girl," he replied. "I always have *that* in mind."

She almost giggled. "Don't I know it! But we have other things to think about."

"Right," he said. "A couple of little things such as…where to live for starters."

"A very little thing," she concurred facetiously.

"That's an easy one, hon. We can live wherever you want, but the closer to Fenway, the better. However, I'm flexible. We both need to be happy."

"I think we can handle that. After all, I work in town, too."

"Right. And then, of course"—he reached for her hand—"we need to choose a date, and a ring."

And suddenly, their romance became as real as his hand stroking hers. So much to plan. To do. Another wedding. Another groom. A different life. Starting over—again. Her stomach plunged. It was all too much, too soon.

"C-can we slow down a little?" She immediately felt the car decelerate, the landscape moving more slowly past them.

"Not the car, Andy. Our lives. Everything's happening so fast now, I'm feeling a bit—ah— overwhelmed."

The glance he gave her this time showed his concern. "Like you're on an express train when you'd rather be taking a local?"

He got her. He always got her. She smiled at him. "Yes. Exactly right. I need more time to smell the roses—so to speak."

"Then we do nothing right now. We can tell your folks we're going forward, but we've got a lot of logistics to figure out. So, no rushing."

"Logistics," she repeated slowly. "Right up my alley. Strategies, plans, tactics, coordination. It covers a lot of stuff that I became very good at while moving around with Matt and watching him work."

Matt's name had come naturally to her in this conversation, but she looked closely to see if Andy noticed, if he'd be annoyed. Oh, she was losing it. Andy wasn't like that at all.

"Well, then," said Andy, "your experience can come in handy for us. We're the ones making plans here, Shannon. No one else. Not your in-laws, not your parents, not my siblings. We hold off until you feel solid ground under your feet again."

"Andrew?"

"Yes."

"Do you realize it's barely more than a month since we reconnected? That's not a lot of time to-to commit to…umm…forever."

"Maybe not for some people," said Andy. "But…well, let's see…. The story goes that my dad fell for my mother the minute they were introduced. And Mike has always said a lightning bolt hit him when Lisa opened that front door to him for the first time. As for Doug – well he was hooked as soon as he read Jen's essay in a freshman English class.

"Compared to them, Shannon, you and I have years behind us. We're just a little older and a bit more bruised since we were last together. You're the same Shannon I've always known and admired. The same Shannon who I now love."

She touched her face where tears had started to roll down her cheeks. He was right. He was simply an older version of the same sweet, talented Andy Delaney he'd been back then. Before they'd gone their separate ways.

"I'm praying my hardest," Andy continued, "that your sudden fears are just normal bridal jitters. So, just forget that express train! We're at the controls here and can roll as slowly as you want."

She detected his tension now. His words had been so calm and comforting, she had almost believed his emotions matched them. But he wasn't calm on the inside. A rapid pulse beat at his neck and his knuckles showed white on the steering wheel.

Her heart opened, and her fears melted. She placed her hand gently over his. "We're fine. I'm fine. That laundry list of tasks and all the changes they represent…suddenly hit me like a tornado. I guess you could call it a reality check."

"I like this reality, Shan. I like it very much."

"Me, too. Let's stop at my folks' place and tell them to expect a new son-in-law in the new year—when we figure it out."

Shannon called first and within an hour, they pulled up to her parents' home on Beacon Street.

"Sorry, kids," said Helen. "Only leftovers today. You missed the big dinner yesterday."

"We didn't come here to eat," said Shannon.

"Speak for yourself, blue-eyes. I don't turn down home cooking no matter what else is going on."

Helen's laugh filled the air. "I like a man who appreciates a good cook."

"Mom—by his standards, even I'm a good cook. So, don't get too excited."

"Well, you haven't poisoned me yet," said Andy, eyes gleaming. "And I'm counting on that skill for many more years to come."

Helen froze for a moment, then motioned to her husband. "Jim—come over here." She looked at Andy. "Want to repeat that?"

"Heck, I'll shout it from the rooftop if you want."

"An-dee! Santa on da rooftop, too!"

Shannon watched Andy sweep Maddie into his arms. "You're so right. But he's not there now. He had to go back to the North Pole. That's where he lives."

Her daughter's face was a picture of concentration before she put her little hands on each of his cheeks. "But you don't go to Norf Pole. You stay here. You stay here wif Mommy and me."

Andy's glance at Shannon held a question, and taking a breath, she slowly nodded. Her parents remained fixed on their granddaughter.

"That's just what I'm going to do, sweetie pie," he said, taking one of her hands and kissing the palm. "I'm going to stay with you and Mommy forever. Is that okay?"

Her eyes widened. "Yes!" Quickly, however, a little frown formed and she looked at Shannon. "Okay, Mommy?"

"Sounds good to me."

Maddie beamed up at Andy. "Okay, Andy." She looked at her Grandma. "Snack time?"

"Just one minute, darling." Helen approached her daughter, while Andy stepped toward Jim and said, "I love her and will do everything I can to make her happy."

"That's only half of it, son. It takes two to make a happy couple." The firm handshake sent its own message of approval.

"And what does my darling daughter say about all this?" asked Helen, cupping Shannon's cheek.

"I'll say to you what I said to Susan this morning...which seems like a lifetime ago now."

Helen's browed raised. "Susan? That was brave."

"Maybe, but secrets don't work. I told her that I got amazingly lucky twice in a lifetime. And I meant every word because it's true."

"The way I see it," said Andy slowly, "is that Matt's part of the family tree, and the tree just grows. I'm not taking Matthew's place. I'm forging my own new branch."

151

"Exactly right," said Shannon, joining him and raising her face to peck his cheek. "How'd you get so smart?"

"Ha! Not smart enough for all our logistics. Why don't you…" He cocked his head toward his soon-to-be in-laws. "I'm sure they'll have ideas."

"Ideas?" asked Helen as she deposited leftovers on the table. "What kind of ideas?"

"Oh, just a few little items like when, where, how, what and who. Like a reporter gathering a story."

"Very apt," said Helen, "in more ways than one. It seems to me that you two both have quite the stories behind you. Thankfully, we're looking at a rainbow ending."

"You've got that absolutely right," said Andy.

##

January provided Andy with time to devote to scouting. Scouting for a ring, a neighborhood, a house and, of course, time to figure out a wedding date that worked for all of them. Of the entire list, the date was proving the hardest. Baseball season could be a bummer. And he didn't want to wait until next fall, almost a whole year away.

"All-Star Week," suggested Brian when Andy called him, the only other person who'd been there, done that and knew baseball as well as Andy. "That's four days off in mid-July. Perfect for a wedding and visitors. You could postpone a real honeymoon. Heck, you've been floating on air anyway."

"Look who's talking," Andy replied.

"And not hiding it," said Brian. "Married is better, bro. Trust me. Married is better—to the right woman, of course. And I think you've got a winner. You two seem like a great match."

"Yeah. I think so, too," said Andy, his voice soft. "So, let's talk about All-Star Week. What if you get picked to play in the game?"

"Or you."

"Shoot. I'd rather get married."

"Not in your contract, I'm afraid," replied Brian. "But look, the game's always on a Tuesday night. So plan the wedding for Wednesday night. Even if one of us plays, we'll get back in time. You'll even have a day to recover before you're back on the road."

"Talk about cutting it close… This can't be normal."

"Compared to what?" Brian asked. "It's normal for the Majors, and as Meggie likes to remind me when I moan about traveling again, I make a damn good living, so I'm not allowed to complain."

Andy chuckled as he pictured feisty Megan giving Brian some sass.

"She does have a point…"

"And it's a fair one. So think about it. And then there's this: ask Shannon! She may have an opinion."

"Just wanted to give her options. I suppose we could wait until October. Which would suck."

"If Boston goes to the World Series, you'll be mentally and physically exhausted anyway in October. Not good for a groom."

"I'll work around anything I have to. Good talking to you, Brian. Hug Josh and kiss Meg and Gracie for me. Talk to you again soon."

He hung up, once more grateful that Brian was his twin brother. They could talk about anything, even weddings. As for Shannon, what he told Brian was true about giving her options. In his scouting role, he'd bring back suggestions and information. Then she could decide what she wanted to do. He was fine with anything.

##

"Next month?" he asked Shannon, in disbelief. Several days after his call to Brian, he sat across from Shannon at her kitchen table in "his" chair while Maddie was playing on the floor, surrounded by blocks, dolls and picture books.

"You should see your expression!" said Shannon between laughs. "Surprised you, have I?"

He nodded. "Surprise? You knocked me out!"

"Well, I can browse a calendar, too," she said. "And I did, marking off the entire baseball season and where you'd be. The only way we can get some time alone is off-season, before you go to Florida for spring training."

"I'm fine with this," said Andy, "more than fine, but I don't understand. A couple of weeks ago, you were overwhelmed just thinking about arrangements."

"I've caught my breath, Andy, and I'm good to go. I'd rather choose a date that works best for us than settle for a date because we can squeeze it in between games."

"You mean, take some time to smell those roses?"

"Exactly. At least, a little more time." She smiled at him with a warmth that went straight to his heart…and other places.

"If we can impose on Mike and Lisa to use their connections with the hotel that ran the gala, how to do feel about a champagne brunch?" Her face was alight; the idea of a brunch seemed to tickle her.

"You're happy with just a brunch? Nothing bigger or more elaborate?"

"A fancy brunch, honey. With shrimp and roast beef as well as the traditional breakfast items. The guests won't be hungry."

"I wasn't concerned about our guests. I'm thinking about you."

She suddenly seemed shy, a bit self-conscious. "A brunch feels right to me." When she looked at him again, she didn't quite meet his gaze.

"I wanted something different." She reached for his hands and intertwined their fingers. Finally, she looked into his eyes. "It's my second walk down the aisle, Andy...so I wanted something unique to us. For Shannon and Andrew. Not a repeat performance, so to speak. But we can change it, if you want the big evening affair?"

He leaned closer to her and captured her lips. "All I want is you. It's a perfect idea."

"And perfect timing," she added with a grin. "It happens to be Valentine's Day weekend."

"Really? That sounds vaguely familiar," said Andy. "Wait a second." When he caught the illusive memory, he started to laugh and handed his phone over to her.

"Want to tell Brian and Meggie they'll be celebrating their anniversary in Boston?"

"Oh my God," she gasped. "All this wasted time trying to figure everything out on my own when I could have just called Meg. She would have cut to the chase in five minutes."

"True. But look at all the fun you've had with the research."

"I might buy a book for baseball dummies," she said.

"No dummies in this house," he said, "right, Maddie?"

"Right." She was a picture of concentration. "Mommy says no trowing balls in da house."

"I almost lost a lamp..." whispered Shannon.

Chuckling, he scooped the child up, and gave her raspberries on her belly. "You are the best, Maddie. I love you so much."

Her little arms tightened around his neck. "Love you!" She remained in place, quietly content against his chest. He slowly rocked her back and forth.

Shannon approached and he felt her soft touch on his arm. "This might be a good time...?" she whispered.

He placed a kiss on Maddie's forehead. "I totally agree... if she doesn't fall asleep."

##

Andy and she had discussed it, of course—the daddy idea. Just waiting for the right time when they were all together, when her active daughter would run out of steam and could enjoy a quiet conversation.

"I not sleeping, Mommy."

"Good, sweetheart. So we can talk now."

The child grinned down at her from Andy's shoulder. "I yike talking, right, Mommy? You say dat!"

"She's got you there," said Andy, his eyes gleaming.

"Guilty as charged." She stroked Maddie's face. "So how about you listen first this time, Maddie? Then you can talk as much as you want."

"Okay."

"So this story is about Mommy and Andy getting married.

"I yike dat story. Andy stay wif us."

"Me, too. I'm glad you remember about it."

"I 'member dat story." She started to squirm. "Down, Andy, peze. I need my book."

She scampered to her room, returned with a Dr. Seuss book and made a beeline to Andy. "Let's sit on your lap."

"Yes, ma'am." He pulled out a chair and accommodated her.

She pointed at the first page. "See, Andy. Da birdy jumps outta da nest. He yooking for his mommy." She now turned a page or two. "Kitten not his mommy. Cow not his mommy. Can't find mommy."

"Or maybe the little bird is lost," said Shannon.

Andy turned the pages and read to the end, changing his voice for each character. "You know what I think, Maddie?"

"What?"

"The mommy finds the little bird because mommies and daddies always find their babies." He leaned close to her ear. "Didn't I find you?"

Maddie's smile went from ear to ear. "Yes! Andy gonna be my daddy. Lily and Laura tol' me."

"They did?"

She nodded decisively. "Yes. At der house."

"I should have hung out with the kids," he said to Shannon, recalling their visit to Jen and Doug a few days earlier.

"You be my daddy, Andy?" asked Maddie.

"You bet I am. I'll try to be the best daddy you can have in the whole world."

"Our little family is growing, sweetheart," said Shannon. "Two plus one, right?"

"Tr-e-e-ee." She stretched the word and held up three fingers. "Mommy, Daddy, and me."

They both put Maddie to sleep in her new bed—with guardrails.

"Big girl bed," the child murmured as her eyes began to close. "Maddie's big girl bed..." She yawned, but kept trying. "Big g... "

In unison, they waited, just watching their little girl breathe. Andy leaned over and placed a kiss on her cheek.

"She's good for the night," whispered Shannon. "Let's go."

The new dad-to-be couldn't have been happier about Maddie, but the night wasn't over.

"Whew, it's been quite the evening," said Shannon, as she led him into the living room and plopped onto the couch. "But a great one."

Andy lowered himself beside her and took her hand. "And there's more."

"Oh? More surprises?" She rolled toward him. "First, just cuddle next to me. I know whatever you have up your sleeve will be wonderful, but let's take a minute and just...connect."

He wrapped his arms around her. "My pleasure. But what I have isn't up my sleeve. It's in my pocket."

"Hmm...new wallet, new phone or old lint," she teased.

He reached for the jeweler's box that had been burning a hole in his pants all evening as he waited for the right time. Maddie took precedence, so he was punting.

"While you were working in the gallery these past weeks, I scouted around and did a little shopping." Man, his hands felt sweaty.

She bolted to a sitting position. "Andrew! You didn't buy a house, did you? That would be...."

"No, no," he said, laughing hard now, all nerves forgotten. "But I did stop by the jewelry store." He took out the box. "If you don't like it, we can exchange it. That's a definite."

He opened it and watched her expression as she looked at the sapphire and diamond ring. The emerald-cut blue stone was flanked by diamond baguettes. Her hand moved to her neck, and she looked at him.

"It's beautiful, Andrew," she whispered. "Simply gorgeous. I wasn't expecting anything like this...in fact, I'd almost forgotten about a ring."

"I know it's not the traditional diamond," he began, his pulse racing like a runaway train. "And if you want tradition...it's okay. But when I saw the sapphires...I immediately thought of you. Your eyes... "

"My eyes are watering right now." She held out her left hand. "I love it, Andy. Especially the part about why you chose it. Please—you put it on."

"Gladly." He took her hand, kissed it and slipped the ring on her fourth finger. "You really almost forgot?" he asked, while she continued to admire the ring.

"Yeah. I-I'm just not used to luxuries. My family grew that business from the ground up, and we didn't live extravagantly. As for the army's pay...not much there. But I've wanted for nothing...except maybe more darkroom supplies."

"I promise you'll have all you need," Andy said. "Your work is as important to you as mine is to me."

"How did I get so lucky?" she asked. "This beautiful ring is like the beautiful life we're going to have. Shiny bright and blue skies." A furrow formed in her brow. "And when storms come?"

He placed her hand in his. "We handle them together."

"Absolutely."

Robert and Grace Delaney
Heaven
The Universe
February 20th...

Dear Mom and Dad,

I'd like you to meet my wonderful wife, Shannon and our lively, adorable daughter, Maddie. The last of your brood has settled down to family life, something I've wanted for a long time. I just had to wait for the right woman—and I finally found her!

We thought it would be a small affair, but wow, your family has grown! Between your kids and all the in-laws plus your generation of aunts, uncles and cousins, as well as some friends, we had over a hundred people. Nothing remains small with the Delaneys!

Both of you will be forever missed...and celebrated. At our champagne wedding brunch, everyone raised a glass, remembering your deep love for each other and for us. We told our stories through tears and laughter and recalled how we leaned on each other all the way, though especially on Mike and Lisa.

You can definitely be proud of those two!

Jen calls us the Delaney-Brennan clan. Your children are each other's best friends and always come through when needed. Emily played Mendelsohn's Wedding March on her violin as Shannon and I walked down the aisle. How many couples have a virtuoso play for them?

You can rest in peace, knowing all your children are fine and accounted for, including me! I'm no longer a child, although I will always be your child. I am at peace, too, and wanted you to know. My life is filled with love. A man can't ask for more than that.

Your son,
Andy

P.S. Brian and I are reporting for spring training in a couple of days. We love facing off during the season because we're in the same town, and the whole family will show up, especially at Fenway. Looking forward to that.

P.P.S. If you happen to meet up with a guy named Matthew Roberts, shake his hand for me.

The night before leaving for Florida, they all slept at the condo, which was now on the market to be sold. It had served Andy well in many ways, including its proximity to the airport, but he was very much looking forward to establishing a new home with Shannon and Maddie, At the desk in the living room, Andy put his pen down and slipped his latest writing into a binder he'd labelled *Letters from a Son.* He'd collected the ones Lisa had saved, recounting his boyhood struggles through the dark times and more recently, he'd updated them with current events. Happy events.

He leaned back, enjoying the unexpected sense of closure. In fact, reveling in it. This part of his story was done. Any further writing efforts would be found in *Beyond the Locker Room.*

He heard Shannon approaching and looked up with a quick smile. The woman caused him to grin all day long.

"And I thought Doug was the writer in the family," she teased, eyeing the binder.

"I'm no competition for him." Rising from his chair, he crossed to her. Her mouth was so kissable, he couldn't resist.

"Umm...good," she said.

"We've got a great adventure ahead of us, honey. You, me, Maddie...and maybe more...?"

She chuckled. "I'm in for that."

The sound of running feet brought Maddie to them. "Maddie's read-y!" she announced, carrying her little suitcase. "Airplane! Forida! Time to go!"

Andy chuckled, then kissed his bride again. "I'm so damn lucky," he said. "All because of you, my love. Some people thought that I preferred playing the field, but that was true only in a stadium. I've simply been waiting. Just waiting to make the greatest catch of my life. And I did."

He kissed her again.

The End

HELLO FROM LINDA

Dear Reader—

Thank you so much for choosing to read *His Greatest Catch*, the fourth book in my brand-new series, *No Ordinary Family*. I hope the story kept you turning the pages as Shannon Roberts and Andy Delaney discovered love for the first and second time around.

The Broken Circle is the fifth story in the series and is really the one that started it all. You'll be reintroduced to the Delaneys, this time during their growing-up years. The spotlight here is on the romance and marriage of Lisa Delaney and Mike Brennan. I originally published this story in 2016 but had no idea I'd wind up developing it into a romance series when the children grew up! A writing career always brings surprises. I hope you'll agree that this was one of the good ones!

An excerpt from *The Broken Circle* follows. You'll also find an excerpt from the first in this series, *Unforgettable*. If you missed Jennifer's story in Book 1, here's your chance to catch up—and it's free!

If you enjoyed reading *His Greatest Catch*, please help others find it so they can discover Linda Barrett books, too. Here's what you can do:

- Write an honest review and post it on Amazon, Barnes & Noble, iBooks, Kobo or any of your favorite book sites. Short is good!
- Keep up with me at my website at: www.linda-barrett.com to find out about upcoming books.
- Sign up for my newsletter on my website.
- Tell your friends! Word of mouth is still the best way to share news about a book you've enjoyed.

I'm sincerely grateful for your help in getting the word out about *His Greatest Catch* and my other novels, which are listed below and available both electronically and in print.

Thank you very much for being a Linda Barrett fan. I truly appreciate you!

Best,
Linda

EXCERPT FROM
UNFORGETTABLE
(NO ORDINARY FAMILY SERIES BOOK ONE)

April—New York

Doug Collins paced the floor of his small apartment in New York City, his eyes drawn repeatedly to the pile of papers on his desk. Two hundred sheets, stacked neat and square, title page on top.

Stepping closer, he loomed over his work. Not the usual fare for a playwright, this novel—but it was finally complete. Finished. His fist came down hard on the manuscript. Finished? Then where was the satisfaction he longed for? Where was the closure? He stroked the top page in atonement and smiled ruefully. Closure? Not with that title:

STRAIGHT FROM THE HEART…
…*a love story in search of an ending…*

He and Jen. How could the story's inspiration be anyone else?

Jennifer Grace Delaney. She was either his inspiration or his albatross. While students together at Boston University, she'd been the quiet girl in the back of the English class who'd captured his heart with her first essay—writing filled with pain, strength, and wrapped in love. Goosebumps had covered his skin as he'd read her words aloud to the class in a random exchange of student essays. They covered him now, as he recalled their honesty. But she'd hated that class. Said personal stories belonged in a private diary, not exposed to a bunch of strangers. She'd stick to numbers.

She'd loved him, too. Believed in him. They'd planned a future…at least he'd thought they had…but in the end, she wouldn't leave her siblings.

His breath jerked at the memory. They could have had the perfect life: Wall Street for Jen; Broadway for him. Or rather off-off Broadway back then. Serious theater. He'd lined up a bartending job at night, too. He'd thought Jen was onboard.

But on the day after graduation, she'd met him in Boston Common with shadowed eyes and a forced smile.

"What's wrong, Henny-Penny?"

Avoiding his gaze, she'd said, "I'm not good at beating around the bush, so I'll just come out with it." She'd finally looked at him. "I've taken the position with Fidelity here in Boston. I can't leave my family. I can't move to New York."

He stared, frozen. "How could you make such an important decision without discussing it first—with me? We're the two that count here."

"I know," she said softly, "but I couldn't take the chance that you'd change my mind. I'm so torn inside. I want to go, but I just can't leave Lisa to manage everything. The boys are a teenage handful and Emily...well, you know sweet Em. Still not the most confident kid on the block."

Her generous heart. He loved her for it, but... "Sometimes, Jen, loyalty can go too far. Your big sister's not alone. There are two adults in that house."

Her mouth wobbled, and she reached for his hand. "Technically, yes. But Mike and Lisa...? I don't know. Something's not right between them. I can feel it. I'm uneasy. They leave notes for each other and don't talk. Mike comes home late often, and I think he's out with his team, hitting some clubs. He never used to do that. He and Lisa..."

She paused, and he saw her gasp for breath.

"...seem to be living two separate lives in one house. I don't know what's happened or what's going to happen, and I-I just can't leave my brothers and sisters now. They're too young. They need me."

Silence pulsed against his ears. "Have you spoken with Lisa directly?"

"I can't," she whispered. "Lisa's so private. She thinks she's protecting us. And really, their marriage isn't my business. Mike's been very good to me. To all of us." She shrugged. "It's just...he's gone so often during the season, and now he's gone at night in the off-season. All I know is that Lisa's got too much on her plate."

"All marriages have tough times. They'll work it out."

"Maybe so," she admitted, "but I know what I see and feel. Threads are fraying—again. She rose from their bench and gazed into the distance. "The timing is wrong for us. But maybe we can find some weekends to visit.

167

It's a short flight, right?" She faced him again, her eyes welling. "Maybe when the kids are older, I'd feel better about leaving them. Please, Doug, please don't argue with me."

Damn! Was she just going to fold like that? She was twenty-two now, a college graduate. An adult.

"What about us, Jen? An occasional weekend is not a real life! You're entitled to your freedom."

Her chin had come up, the threat of tears gone, her violet eyes now almost sizzling black. "Am I really? After everything she's given up for us—me and the little ones? I-I can't leave her to cope alone. I'm the next oldest. I love them, and I...owe them!"

His blood ran hot, but his stomach knotted in cold fear. If he was going to lose this argument, he wouldn't go down easy.

"Can't leave them or won't? Tell me, Jen, for how many years does the accident reverberate? For how many years is it allowed to control you? You're the math genius, so what's the answer?"

She froze for a moment, then cupped his cheek. "You already know the answer," she whispered. "Deep inside...that place where truth lives."

He flinched now as he recalled her words. His words. He'd used them on her after reading that essay, the one that had blown him away.

Now the tears ran down her cheek as she spoke. "I'm so sorry, Doug. I'm sorry for us both. But my family has to come first. The Delaney siblings either stick together or fall. That's what I've learned. If we'd been separated back then, after the accident...well, we wouldn't have survived, not as a family." She kissed him quickly. "It won't be forever. Maybe one day, you'll be able to write again in Boston. We'll talk on the phone. We'll visit on weekends."

He knew she was grasping for a thread of salvation, but he was, too. "I love you, Jen. Don't disappear on me."

Then she'd kissed him and run off, leaving him to stare in disbelief.

He rubbed his damp forehead as the image of a racing Jennifer, long hair flying, remained in his mind's eye. The emotions remained, too. Love, disappointment, anger, frustration—he'd wanted to smash something. Writing a scene, he'd discovered, was a hell of a lot easier than living through one.

Patting the manuscript on his desk, he collapsed into the chair in front of the computer.

He'd called Jen every Sunday in the beginning. She flew down once, met a couple of his friends—other writers. He'd hoped to change her mind, convince her to take a chance in the Big Apple. "You could have stayed in Boston," she'd countered. But that wasn't true. Not with his hard-won residency with Playwrights' House— an opportunity of a lifetime.

The visits became fewer, the phone calls less frequent. Busy careers. Busier lives. Both trying to make their marks.

But dammit! Five years in limbo was long enough!

He tapped the keyboard and composed an email to his friend, editor Steven Kantor. The man was doing him a favor by reading a manuscript not for publication. Steve wouldn't earn a dime, even if he loved it. But maybe that's what goosed the editor's curiosity. He knew Doug's plays—his emergence as a serious playwright—heck, the guys had been friends for five years, hitting New York at about the same time, both craving success and working non-stop.

"If you wrote it," Steve had said, "it won't be a time-waster. Just send it when you're ready. Maybe I'll learn something."

A compliment like that couldn't be bought. Doug gifted him with tickets to any Broadway show he wanted.

He skimmed the manuscript pages one more time. Then, attaching the electronic file to his email, he took a deep breath and hit Send.

It was time to let Jen go. Or find her again.

##

One month later—Boston

On a late Friday afternoon in May, Jennifer Delaney hung up the phone—hopefully the last call of the day—and walked to her office window, amazed, as always, at how lucky she'd been. A wonderful career, great friends...not to mention the stunning view of Boston Harbor.

The huge investment firm where she worked suited her to a T. Helping to manage funds and advising clients about risk soothed their money worries as well as her own. Sighing, she acknowledged how ridiculous that seemed now. Her checkbook, her personal investments were sound. She wondered why childhood scars were so hard to heal.

Losing loving parents at sixteen...unspeakable pain. But she'd survived. Her older sister and brother-in-law thought she'd thrived. Her younger siblings thought she was cool. Maybe she was! Regardless, they'd had each other's backs from the beginning of those rough days and always would. She couldn't imagine her life without them. Her life was good. Calm. Balanced. Like her checkbook. "Just the way I want it to be," she murmured.

Her phone rang again. Shaking her head, she raced back to her desk. "Jennifer Delaney speaking."

"How are you, Henny-Penny?"

That voice. The receiver slipped from her hand and hit the floor. That warm voice. That nickname. Once upon a time...

Retrieving the phone, she said, "I'm well. Doing very well, thanks. It's been a long time...so, how's New York?"

"New York was humming along the last I saw it. And that's the thing, Jen. I'm back in Boston now, and I'd love to see you. Any chance you're free tonight? The workday's almost over."

Back in Boston? Like forever or just a quick visit? Their parting might have been her decision years ago, but the pain afterward? She couldn't go through that kind of heartache again, she decided. Better to bail quickly.

"Sorry, I've already got plans for tonight. But I hope you enjoy your visit."

She disconnected and took a deep breath. She'd been polite, her voice steady. Good job. When the phone rang again, she glanced at the readout, took another—deeper—breath before answering. "Let's blame a poor connection. I've got plans for tonight," she repeated.

"How about tomorrow? Saturday."

She gripped the receiver as though it were a life preserver. "Afraid not. I'm booked."

"Is that right?"

"In fact, I'm looking at my calendar right now," she said, with a quick glance at it, "and every day has something scheduled. I'm sorry, but I've really gotta go. As I said before, have a nice visit."

Replacing the phone gently in the cradle, she shivered. A whole body shiver. She hadn't lied. Her life was busy—and calm—just the way she liked it. She and Doug had simply drifted apart, following their own paths in their own worlds. At this point, she didn't need any emotional upheavals. She studied her computer screen, and in minutes, she was once again Jennifer Delaney, happy career woman.

##

At five-thirty, Jen was surrounded by co-workers who'd become friends, all set to kick back and hit the clubs. That's what twentysomethings did on a Friday night in Boston. And she loved a good time as much as anyone.

"I'm just about ready," she said, smiling, as she logged out of her computer. They stood outside her office door—two guys and two gals—all trying to prove themselves, but still believing the theory about all work and no play. Her friends were certainly not dull. Not these bright, energetic, career-minded people. They were her friends for a reason!

She changed her high heels for flat sandals, grabbed her purse, rose and joined the others. "I'm hungry. Where are we eating?"

Alexis laughed, her brown eyes shining. "You mean we're not sampling the freebies at every bar's happy hour and saving on dinner?"

"Oh, geez. I'm not that bad, am I?" Jen protested.

Her friends simply stared. "When it comes to spending money, let's just say—you're frugal," said Alexis.

She held up her hands. "Okay, okay...guilty as charged."

"Not that we're complaining," chimed in Liz, with a chuckle. "Living in Beantown is expensive, and saving is a challenge."

"Well, I'm conceding right now," said Matthew. "Some of us need real food! Not just peanuts."

"Then go home to your mama, and get a good meal," said Liz, reaching up to pat him on the shoulder.

Everyone laughed as they piled into the elevator, but Jen sensed new vibes. Matt and Liz. The young woman's gentle teasing, her tender touching was becoming a habit.

The elevator deposited them in the spacious marble lobby of the building, and the group headed toward the plate glass doors leading to the plaza outside.

"The days are getting longer and warmer," said Matt, holding the door open for the others, "which means our playtime is longer, too."

The chatter continued, but when Jen stepped outside, she heard nothing more, and saw nothing except the tall man with a hank of dark hair falling over his forehead, the man whom she'd once labeled skinny but wasn't anymore, the man who'd once held her heart. Surprise held her frozen until a slow anger warmed her up.

She watched him, and by his stillness, identified the moment he spotted her. One second, two seconds. He waited, but made no move toward her, as though afraid she'd disappear.

Then came the smile, the smile that once had melted her heart. She used to run her fingers over his mouth, outlining his lips, kissing them. But that was then...

Her hands clenched into fists as he finally approached. She moved closer to her friends.

"Hang on a sec," she whispered, her throat dry.

They halted instantly.

"What's wrong, Jen?"

She couldn't speak. Doug was only six feet from them now, filling her vision. And suddenly, he was there. Right in front of her.

"Hello, Jennifer Grace Delaney. I've missed you."

No! Taller, bigger than in her memory. And his eyes, still so dark, darker than a moonless night is how she used to think of them. A kaleidoscope of remembrances hit her at once, and her initial anger ebbed, replaced by an eon of past loneliness and disappointment. And right now, fear. She wouldn't survive a repetition of the past.

"Who is this guy?" Her four friends surrounded her.

She gulped some air, raised her chin. "Someone I used to know. An old college...uh...classmate."

Her friends were astute. Their eyes focused on him, then Jen, their curiosity apparent. He didn't care about her friends—what they saw, heard or thought. Only Jen was real. And more beautiful than in his dreams.

"An old classmate, huh?" he repeated. "That's a funny way to describe what we had." He focused on her face. "This guy," he said, echoing her friend's question, "is the man who can't forget you."

Her eyelids slammed shut, her mouth trembled before tightening. When she opened her eyes again, however, her gaze was steady. "It's been years, Doug. As the saying goes, 'that was then, this is now.' Maybe you need to try harder to...ah...forget."

"I've moved back, Jen."

"No, no, you haven't," she countered, her surprise laced with confusion. Returning didn't make sense at all. "Playwrights live in New York. We tried once, and it didn't work. I'm sorry, Doug, but I've moved on. She turned toward her friends. "It's time to leave. We're all starving."

Not yet. Not without him. He held out both hands, palms up. "Eight million people in New York," he said, slightly bouncing his left hand. "And one Henny-Penny here." He lifted his right arm high. "No contest."

She shrugged. "You didn't think so back then. You're very good with words, images and make-believe. While I, in case you've forgotten, deal with real people."

"I know."

She stepped toward him, her purse falling to the ground, her friends closing ranks behind her. "Real people, Collins, like the Delaney family. Not your ordinary kind of family. Just a bunch of kids trying to survive."

Good. Talk to me. Keep on talking. Communication is everything.

Before he could say a word, she turned to her friends again. A girl handed her the purse. "Sorry for the drama," Jen said. "It's the way he makes his living. He's good at it."

"Him? What about you?" a guy said. "A new side of the mysterious Jennifer Delaney."

So, he'd gotten to her, past her defenses. He wanted to cheer. The men were merely co-workers. If they thought of her as mysterious, she'd kept her private life private. Which meant no boyfriends. Regardless of what she'd said earlier, she hadn't moved on.

Which gave him hope.

Now all he needed was a little *chutzpah* to make his next move and be accepted by Jen's friends. "I remember a great club near here," he said, deliberately placing himself in the middle of the group. "Lots of eats, lots of music, and a karaoke bar."

Jen had turned away, but he saw her stiffen. Tapping her on the shoulder, he said, "You know we'll have fun. At least a song or two. Come on, Jen...I dare you."

##

175

Dare her? Like in the old days, except those were happy times with music and a microphone. Right now, she wanted the privacy of her own apartment. She needed to regain her equilibrium, to brace herself for whatever came next. But if she left, Doug would accuse her of running away. Again.

Pasting a smile on her face, Jen said, "All that goofing around in college? Nah. I don't do that anymore."

She threw a speaking glance at her girlfriends. They loved to kick back at the sing-along karaoke bars. Jen had the real voice, but they all had fun. Now, however, she knew her pals would cover for her.

"Then prove it," said Doug.

"What?"

He was shaking his head. "You always enjoyed being on a cozy stage. I can't believe you've changed that much. And you're good! Let's go to a club, Jen. For old times' sake. After all, I am new in town…."

"Oh, pu-leeze," she shot back. "You know this city like a native."

"It's been a few years."

She turned to the others. "I'm sorry about all this. Do you mind if we skip the pubs and go right to Maguire's? Real food for the starving plus live music, and then I'll go home. I've got an early choir rehearsal tomorrow anyway."

"I don't like this situation," said Evan, a quiet type who missed nothing. "Just say the word, Jen, and we'll get rid of…"

Oh, no! She patted the man's arm. "I'm fine, Evan. Really. He's not dangerous, except with a pen!" She smiled at him. "But thanks."

Five years building a life, and in five minutes, Doug Collins could tear it down. She couldn't chance another disappointment. Why had he come back after all this time? Glancing at her watch, she sighed. One hour or so was all she'd have to endure.

The Irish bar was filling up, but they managed to get a booth for six immediately. Jen sighed again, happy with their good luck, happy to keep to her one-hour plan.

Almost as immediately, Doug seemed comfortable with the group and made her friends feel comfortable with him. Not surprising. He had always been the proverbial "people person." She'd credit his many psychology courses.

Evan's quiet voice, however, managed to interrupt the general conversation about the menu and music. "So, Collins, what brings you back to Boston?"

A curious silence descended, and for the first time, Doug seemed to search for words. Jen's ears perked up.

"Let's say," he began slowly, "a couple of new projects and one item of unfinished business. Very important unfinished business." From diagonally across the table, he shifted toward Jen, his eyes capturing hers.

She sat straighter. "If you mean me, you're mistaken," she said, leaning forward, arms on the table. "Our 'business,' as you call it, is over. Nothing personal—though I guess you'd think it was—but I'm not looking for a relationship with you or anyone else. Just not my thing." *Not anymore.*

The quality of the following silence morphed from curious to deafening. She realized that in all her years with the company, she'd revealed more about herself just then than ever before. And now to prevent speculation—and gossip—she'd have to explain.

She glanced around the table, finding sympathy laced with curiosity in her friends' expressions. Okay.

She could handle that. Her message, however, was meant for Doug. She returned her gaze to him.

"In my world," she began, "people leave. First my parents—and you have no idea what that was like—and then you, and I wasn't sure about Mike and Lisa staying together either. I know you have to accept what's out of your control, like a car accident on an icy road. But I'm not going to volunteer for more heartache and grief. My life is great as it is. Your being in Boston is totally immaterial to me."

"Then it seems," he said softly, "that I have a lot of work to do."

The waitress approached, and conversation turned to food and drink. "Just a cup of chicken soup," said Jen. "I've lost my appetite."

"Maybe him tagging along wasn't a good idea," said Evan, nodding toward Doug. "You've managed to upset Jen, who's a very cool woman. So, let's get the whole picture. Why else are you here? What kind of projects?"

Jen looked at her co-worker. Who would have thought that this quiet guy would speak up now? Still waters....?

Doug shifted in his seat. His gaze swept both sides of the booth. "I'm a writer. I worked hard and got lucky, too. I have a new play, and its debut will be here with the Commonwealth Regional Theater company. And that's as far as I'm thinking."

Jen heard nothing after Commonwealth. Her choir, The All-City Chorus, rehearsed at that theater twice a week, and she'd be there in the morning. "'Of all the gin joints...'" she murmured.

She'd never doubted his talent, and she'd been right. His very first play had been staged in college. A rare honor. He'd been thrilled, of course, but shy about it. He used to say that writers were too insecure to brag.

And now, he'd been modest in front of her friends. It seemed he'd been totally focused on his craft while living in New York.

"Congratulations," she offered. "Sounds like you'll be busy with rehearsals and whatever—for a little while, and after a successful run here, poof! Back to Broadway. Works well for me."

"Writing your own script, Jen?" Doug's eyes gleamed. "Sorry to disappoint. I didn't renew the lease on my New York apartment because….I'm also this year's playwright-in-residence at our alma mater. If *The Sanctuary* goes to Broadway, I'll commute."

She needed air.

"I'm back, Jen. And tomorrow I'm hunting for new digs. I can't stay with my sister indefinitely. Any suggestions?" His glance traveled from Jen to the others, and she sighed in relief at the change of topic. An objective, neutral topic. Boston sported a dozen or more neighborhoods attractive to singles.

"It really depends on your budget," said Liz. "In this town, a one-bedroom can run anywhere from sixteen hundred to double that a month."

"I'd like to be close to the theater, if possible."

"Then that would be downtown," said Evan slowly. "A great choice."

Could the night get any worse? First the theater, now Jen's neighborhood—a walking neighborhood where she could run into him at any time. "I doubt he can afford it."

In unison, all eyes turned toward first toward her, then toward Doug.

"She's got a point, man," said Even. "But there are other great locations."

"There sure are," said Jen calmly now. "Many good areas. You don't need to be downtown."

Doug's eyes narrowed. "Any particular reason, Henny-Penny?"

Liz coughed and hid her mouth. Matt looked away. Not a shred of acting material in them.

"No reason at all." Jen waved her arm in dismissal. "Search the whole city. Means nothing to me if you go into debt." Deflection might work.

"For crying out loud, I might have known," said Doug with a sigh. "The starving playwright thing.... Well, I'm not quite there, and you don't have to worry I'll be asking for a loan. I do know how to budget." He chuckled and looked around the table, making eye contact with each person for a moment. "Although I seem to be in a minority among the financial whizzes here."

Everyone laughed. "Financial whizzes believe in budgets, too," said Liz.

"Who knows?" Doug said. "One day soon, I might be asking for advice."

And that's when Jen knew that Doug had turned her friends into his friends, too.

EXCERPT FROM
THE BROKEN CIRCLE
(NO ORDINARY FAMILY SERIES BOOK FIVE)

January 1995
Boston

A knock at her grad school apartment door pulled Lisa
Delaney away from Commonwealth of Massachusetts
vs. Torcelli Construction. Eyes burning, she rubbed her
lids while, from her iPod, she heard Bryan Adams insist
that everything he did, he did for her. Old song. Easy
words. If the man really wanted to impress, he could
take her contracts exam in the morning.

She pushed away from her desk, covered in law
books and case briefs, and rose from her chair,
stretching, bending and groaning. Her knees creaked like
an arthritic old lady's. Shaking her head, she emitted a

long sigh and promised herself a gym visit the next day—after the exam.

A second knock echoed, this time more impatiently

"I'm coming. Hang on." Nimble again, she rushed across the room and opened the door.

Her eyes widened, her stomach began to roil as she looked at two uniformed state troopers, snow melting on their jackets, cop faces in place. Her thoughts raced with possibilities. Classmates? Mike? Oh, please, not Mike.

"Are you Lisa Delaney?"

She stared at bad news and froze. All of her. Nothing worked. Not her mind, tongue, or breath. Perhaps her heart had stopped, too. One man coughed. The other repeated the question.

"I-I'm Lisa."

"Are your parents' names Robert and Grace Delaney?"

Oh, God, yes! Her heart raced at Mach speed, but she couldn't feel her legs at all. "What happened?"

"May we come in, Ms. Delaney?" Taller cop.

She nodded and pulled the door wider, but the knob slipped through her sweaty hands and she lost her balance.

"You might want to sit down."

As though moving underwater, she struggled into the closest chair.

"I'm afraid there's been an accident on the turnpike," began the quiet-till-now officer. "A fatal accident."

"Not…not my…my parents?" She barely got the words out before the officers' sympathetic silence answered her question.

"But that's impossible! I just spoke to my dad…"

"When was that, ma'am?"

When? When? "I think…maybe…last…last night…." Her voice drifted. Daddy had been checking up on his eldest, his numero uno child, joking with her about an apple a day. Staying healthy. A convenient excuse to call. To keep in touch with the one who'd left home. She'd understood his M.O. a month after arriving at school. Sweet, loving man. A man with a phone.

"Wh-what...?" Her throat closed.

The cops seemed to understand her intent. "The official investigation is ongoing, but according to preliminary reports, the other driver lost control of his vehicle and did a one-eighty."

"Drunk? But...but it's the middle of the week." As if that fact could change things.

"The driver's blood alcohol was normal."

"Then what...? The road...?"

"Icy conditions contributed. The temperature drops at night, and your folks were approaching at just the wrong moment. There were no survivors. I'm very sorry."

She nodded. *No survivors? Mom and Dad?* She wanted to cover her ears.

The other officer looked at his notes and said, "The Woodhaven police are with your brothers and sisters."

Oh, God, the kids... She had to get back to Woodhaven!

Standing quickly, she was hit by a wave of nausea and fell back into her chair. She doubled over, hand on her stomach. The phone rang, startling her further. She stared at the instrument, half-buried by textbooks, reached forward, and slowly lifted the receiver. "Hello?" she whispered.

"Lisa! Lisa! The police are here. Mom and Dad were in an accident. You have to come home! Now! I'm scared."

Jennifer. Her social butterfly teenage sister whose life revolved around boyfriends, best friends, and having fun. Except, not tonight. In the background, she heard the cacophony of younger voices crying and talking at the same time. She heard little Emily's high-pitched wail. "When is Lisa coming?"

"Hang on, Jen." She took a breath and looked at the officers. "There are four of them. Emily's only seven. My twin brothers are nine. Jen's sixteen. I've got to get there—a hundred miles—and I don't own a car." She couldn't afford one and didn't need one in a city with mass transit.

The troopers nodded, and she spoke into the phone again.

"I'll be there soon, Jen. As soon as I can. Maybe William and Irene can stay with you meanwhile." Her fiancé's parents lived across the street.

"They're not home. They went to Miami to see Mike play. Didn't you watch the game yesterday?"

"Of course I watched, but I didn't know his folks flew down." Mike had subbed for the starting quarterback and played an entire quarter. It was only his first year, but now the Riders were in the play-offs.

"So, Jen, you need to be in charge now until I get there. You and the kids sit tight and wait for me." She glanced toward the window, where falling snow was reflected by the light of the streetlamps.

"It might take a little while," she added. "It's a big trip, and the roads are bad..." What was she saying? Her parents had just been killed on those roads. "Jen, honey, let me talk to one of the officers there."

Her hand shook as she gave the receiver to the state cop. "Ask if they told the kids the truth."

In seconds, he shook his head. "Not yet. They're getting a social worker in on it."

She raised her eyes to his. "Please tell them not to do or say anything until I get there. Okay?"

Perspiration trickled from every pore. She shivered and sweated until finally her stomach lurched. Running into the bathroom, she vomited until nothing remained. Then she brushed her teeth, packed her suitcase to the brim, and snapped it shut. The sound focused her, and she inhaled a deep breath. *Be strong, be strong...*

One of the troopers held the door open. Her gaze skimmed the small apartment. She'd been happy there and ecstatic at being accepted into the program. She glanced at her textbooks before locking on to her college graduation photo. Her parents stood on either side of her, their smiles wide.

"Oh-h... One second." Her own future was now uncertain. Dropping her suitcase, she darted to the wall, took down the picture, and tucked it under her arm. Their dreams and her dreams might have to wait awhile.

#

Michael Brennan needed three days to get home to Woodhaven and to Lisa. It seemed like three years.

He tossed his luggage in his parents' front hall, turned around, and headed directly across the street. The Delaneys lived in a two-story wood-framed house with a front porch similar to his and to all the other homes on Hawthorne Street. He'd grown up there, but Lisa and her family had moved in over four years ago in June, right after her high school graduation. He'd graduated from a neighboring high school that same year. Their paths hadn't crossed until the evening his mother baked a cake and insisted their family welcome the new neighbors. Moaning and groaning, he'd given in, and the Brennans had gone to visit the Delaneys.

When Lisa opened the door and walked outside, he'd almost tripped up the front steps. One glance and he couldn't speak. His brain froze, too, as if a lightning bolt had slammed him head to toe. Big violet eyes, long, dark wavy hair, and a killer smile. A friendly smile. *Who*

185

wouldn't have fallen in love with her? But he'd been the lucky one, the lucky guy who'd relished every single day since Lisa Delaney had first appeared at that front door.

Now her sidewalk needed shoveling. The streets had been plowed since the storm a few days ago, the walkways, too, but snow had fallen again yesterday, and surfaces had turned icy. He flexed his shoulders and entered the house. He'd take care of the snow after he wrapped his arms around her…if he could find her.

The Delaney house was packed. He recognized Lisa's aunts and uncles from out of -town, and all the neighbors, of course. Lisa's closest friends, Sandy and Gail, were there, too. Either they'd stayed all day or had just come from work. He waved and searched for his mom.

"Where's Lisa?"

"I'm glad you're here, Michael," she said, giving him a quick kiss, "but don't expect too much from Lisa. She's overwhelmed as…as we all are." Irene Brennan gazed up at the ceiling, indicating the second floor. "She's got the kids with her. The funeral's tomorrow, and she wants time alone with them."

"Alone doesn't include me."

He took the stairs two at a time, sensing the glances, the sympathy of the visitors as he made his way up. He appreciated their support, but they didn't have to worry. Surely, he could handle whatever he found. Surely, he and Lisa could handle it together.

He paused in the hallway at the top of the stairs. Each of the four bedroom doors stood ajar, but he could hear nothing. He started to push the first door open when, from the end of the corridor, he heard Lisa singing quietly, "Too-ra Loo-ra Loo-ra, Too-ra loo-ra lie…"

Was she trying to put the kids to sleep at five o'clock in the afternoon? He slowed his pace and walked the last few steps before knocking softly and entering the master bedroom. Lisa sat on her parents' bed, leaning against the headboard, the twins dozing on either side of her, little Emily sleeping on her lap. Jennifer lay across the foot of the bed, also sound asleep. He took it all in and understood that day and night had no meaning to them.

"Lisa..." A whispered prayer.

Her red-rimmed eyes brightened, her arms opened, and he was there. Kissing her and gently shifting one little brother lower on the mattress. She began to cry, her tears mingling with his as he rained kisses, and his tension melted simply by holding her in his arms. Tears flowed as he continued to embrace her and grieve while remembering Grace and Robert Delaney.

They'd been wonderful neighbors, wonderful parents, and good friends with his folks. The Delaneys had worked so hard to finally become "owners" instead of "renters," and celebrated their move to Hawthorne Street each time they'd made a mortgage payment. Lisa had told him how her dad would brandish the check and twirl Grace around the kitchen every single month. With their growing family, it had taken them fifteen years to afford their own home.

"How long can you stay?" Lisa whispered.

"He can't," mumbled nine-year-old Andy, rousing slightly. "He has to go to the conference championship game. And maybe to the Super Bowl."

"But not yet," Mike said, rubbing the boy's head with affection, but focusing his gaze on Lisa. "I'll be here for the funeral tomorrow. You won't be alone. Then I'll be back in a week. One short week." Which might feel like an eternity to Lisa.

"I'm glad, but-but everything has changed," she said, pulling a tissue from the nearby box and blotting her face. "We need to rethink our plans."

"The basics haven't changed," he replied quickly. "I love you, Lisa Delaney. And don't you forget it."

Her eyes shone. She pressed his hand, her fingers narrow and delicate around his broader ones. "I love you, too, but-but…." She sighed and glanced at the assorted children. "I'm not sure what's going to happen next," she said quietly.

"I am," he said. "I'm going to kiss you again."

And he did. When she kissed him back, when she lingered and leaned against him, he almost collapsed with relief. She was *the one* for him. No matter what. Her needs, the kids' needs….

"We'll sort it out when the time comes," he said. "I'll support you in every way I can." The logistics would no doubt be complicated, but he had faith that he and Lisa could do anything as long as they did it together.

She offered a wan smile. "I know you'll do your best, but you have commitments to the team. You're so talented! We all know you're being groomed as a starting quarterback, maybe even next year. So I think, for both our sakes, I need to handle this-this family situation by myself."

No, she didn't, but her brave effort tore a corner of his heart. "I think you're right about my place in the team," he said slowly, "but that's in our favor. The money's good." He'd worked hard with his coaches, and his natural talents had been recognized. His dream career loomed just over the horizon.

"I must be weird," said Lisa. "I never think about your salary. Even your first year minimum is like make-believe Monopoly money to me. It doesn't matter. I'm just so…so proud of you."

Men cry. Even big football players. But once that afternoon was enough. His throat ached as he swallowed to stem more tears. Lisa needed him to be strong.

"Have I ever told you about my conversation with your dad at the end of the summer you moved to Hawthorne Street?" he asked. "It was right before I went off to Ohio State on my scholarship."

"All Daddy told me was that you were too big for your britches, but he was laughing."

A surge of love and a wave of sadness—both raced through Mike. The words sounded exactly like something Rob Delaney would say. And the laughter—well, laughter was the norm in Lisa's family. Her dad loved to tell a good story and could imitate the comedy greats and their jokes. Rob had been a natural "on stage," and no one had a bigger heart.

"Before I left for college," Mike continued, "I told him I was going to marry you someday."

"You've got to be kidding! We were only eighteen. We'd just met that very summer." For a moment, her expression lightened. She tipped her head back, and her eyes met his. "And what did he say?"

"He said that I'd better treat you like gold—always. And I promised I would."

"O-o-h...." Despair once again etched her face. "Our lives... everything..."—she waved her arm— "has changed. I can't-I *won't* hold you to any promise."

"You have no vote." He kissed her again, vowing to keep that promise. Loving Lisa was the easy part. Building a solid future together...well, that goal might be more difficult to reach now. Lisa was in no condition to make any decisions. Their next steps would be decided by him.

His gaze rested on each of the youngsters, one at a time. Four sweet, innocent children. Without warning, his heart started to race, and his palms became covered in sweat. Fear. Like Lisa, he was almost twenty-three, and deep down, he was scared, too. He had no experience with kids, not even a younger brother or

189

sister. But he wouldn't give himself away, wouldn't let Lisa know. A quarterback led with confidence on the field. Now he had to do the same at home.

LINDA BARRETT BOOKS

NOVELS—ROMANCE

No Ordinary Family Series
Unforgettable (Bk. 1)

Safe at Home (Bk. 2)

Heartstrings (Bk. 3)

His Greatest Catch (Bk. 4)

The Broken Circle (Bk. 5)

Starting Over Series

True-Blue Texan (Bk 1)

A Man of Honor (Bk. 2)

Love, Money and Amanda Shaw (Bk.3)

The Inn at Oak Creek (Bk.4)

Flying Solo Series

Summer at the Lake (Bk. 1)

Houseful of Strangers (Bk. 2)

Quarterback Daddy (Bk. 3)

The Apple Orchard (Bk. 4)

Pilgrim Cove Series

The House on the Beach (Bk. 1)

No Ordinary Summer (Bk. 2)

Reluctant Housemates (Bk. 3)

The Daughter He Never Knew (Bk. 4)

Sea View House Series

Her Long Walk Home (Bk. 1)

Her Picture-Perfect Family (Bk. 2)

Her Second-Chance Hero (Bk. 3)

NOVELS—WOMEN'S FICTION

The Broken Circle

The Soldier and the Rose

Family Interrupted

For Better or Worse – A boxed set of all three WF novels at a discounted price

SHORT NOVELLA

Man of the House

MEMOIR

HOPEFULLY EVER AFTER: Breast Cancer, Life and Me (true story about surviving breast cancer twice)

Printed in Great Britain
by Amazon